Kiska

Books by John Smelcer

Fiction

Stealing Indians
The Gospel of Simon
Savage Mountain
Edge of Nowhere
Lone Wolves
The Trap
The Great Death
Alaskan: Stories from the Great Land

Native Studies

The Raven and the Totem
A Cycle of Myths
Trickster
The Day That Cries Forever
Durable Breath
Native American Classics
We are the Land, We are the Sea

Poetry

Indian Giver
The Indian Prophet
Songs from an Outcast
Riversong
Without Reservation
Beautiful Words
Tracks
Raven Speaks
Changing Seasons

A Novel

JOHN SMELCER

Kiska

Leapfrog Press
Fredonia, New York

Published in 2017 in the United States by
Leapfrog Press LLC
PO Box 505
Fredonia, NY 14063
www.leapfrogpress.com

Printed in the United States of America

Distributed in the United States by
Consortium Book Sales and Distribution
St. Paul, Minnesota 55114
www.cbsd.com

First Edition

Library of Congress Cataloging-in-Publication Data

Names: Smelcer, John E., 1963- author.
Title: Kiska : when her people need a hero, a young girl rises to the challenge / by John Smelcer.
Description: First edition. | Freedonia, NY : Leapfrog Press, 2017. |
Summary: In 1942, when 881 Aleuts are evacuated to an internment camp nearly 2,000 miles away, fourteen-year-old Kiska stands up against the injustice and secretly becomes their champion. | Includes bibliographical references.
Identifiers: LCCN 2017035677 (print) | LCCN 2017017470 (ebook) | ISBN 9781935248941 (epub) | ISBN 9781935248934 (paperback : alk. paper)
Subjects: LCSH: Aleuts--Juvenile fiction. | CYAC: Aleuts--Fiction. | Eskimos--Fiction. | Concentration camps--Fiction. | World War, 1939-1945--Concentration camps--United States. | Alaska--History--1867-1959--Fiction. | Admiralty Island (Alaska)--History--20th century--Fiction.
Classification: LCC PZ7.S6397 (print) | LCC PZ7.S6397 Kis 2017 (ebook) | DDC
[Fic]--dc23
LC record available at https://lccn.loc.gov/2017035677

for Unangan. Xristuusax!

"Everyone knows that Japanese Americans were interned during World War II, but few know of the injustices suffered by the Aleuts of Alaska."
—U. S. Senator Ted Stevens (R-AK)

This is a work of fiction based on historical events and on the testimony of the people who survived it. It is meant to be representative of the Aleut internment experience, not that of a single individual, family, or group. Except for variations in time and character identification and placement, most of the events written in this story are true and actually happened.

The author thanks Bard Young, Steve McDuff, Rod Clark and Melanie Werth, Amber Johnson, Dan Johnson, and John Nash for their editorial advice. He would also like to thank Mike Rosenberg (Passenger) for his album, *All the Little Lights*, the only music he listened to (obsessively) while writing this book. A special thanks to the Starbucks baristas at Hy-Vee who created a warm atmosphere while writing this book. The author would especially like to thank the Aleut elders he interviewed during the mid '80s and early '90s at Alaska Federation of Natives (AFN) conferences held in Anchorage and Fairbanks. This novel is informed by their candid and heartrending stories.

Contents

Kiska

CHAPTER 1
A Distant Thunder

Pour me another cup of tea and sit down, Granddaughter.

I have a story to tell you.

No, that's not what I mean. I *have* to tell you a story. It happened to me when I was about your age. It's a part of history that's not in any of the history books you study at school. It's a story about what happened to our village and all the people who lived here a long time ago. It's about my mother and father, grandmother and uncle, and about my brother and my sister and her baby. It's also about the wisest man I ever knew. I guess it's also a story about me because I'm in it, and I know what happened because I was there and I have a good memory. They say good stories are told from the heart, for the heart. I don't know about that. The story I'm about to tell you has been breaking my heart for such a long time. It may be hard for you to bear. I'm going to tell it just the way it happened because I never forget and I never lie. My mother always told me not to tell lies.

Are you comfortable? Do you want another piece of

cake before I begin? No? Then I will start at the beginning where most stories begin.

· · · ·

The calendar on the wall in our little house said it was June 4, 1942. I remember because I was marking off days until my fourteenth birthday only a few days away. The only other thing hanging on the bare white walls was a cross, which my mother dusted and kissed every day.

Late that morning, I was gathering seagull eggs on the high cliffs above our village when I saw four *baidarkas* approaching on the sea. That's what we call kayaks in our language. I waved and jumped up and down, trying to get the attention of the returning hunters, but I don't think they saw me through the drifting fog. It is always foggy or cloudy or rainy on our island, and the constant wind scours the rugged land. Almost nothing grows but dwarf shrubs and grasses and sedges. There are no trees for a thousand miles; they can't endure the battering winter storms—called *williwaws*—that blow in from the Bering Sea. The cliff tops are so high that on rare clear days when the sky is steep and barren, you can see the endless ocean bend to the curve of the earth. You may think it bleak, but it's beautiful to us. It's our home. We Aleuts have lived on these islands for ten thousand years. In fact, the word for Alaska comes from our language—*Alaxsxa*, which means "Mainland."

With the egg basket in hand, I ran down the grassy footpath toward our village of a dozen or so small hous-

16

es huddled around a white church on the only flat place above the rocky beach.

"Kiska! Come here!" my mother shouted from an open window when I passed near our house. "Be careful with them eggs! You could break them running like that!"

I glanced at the basket. Not a single egg was broken.

"But I saw father and uncle coming around the point," I said. "I want to go see if they caught any seals."

"Leave the basket here."

By the time I got to the beach, the four kayaks were just arriving. As the bows touched the gravel beach, the men climbed out and dragged their crafts ashore. All four stretched after sitting and paddling for so long.

"Did you get a seal?" I asked my father.

Without saying a word Father nodded at a dead seal tied to the back of his kayak, its sleek body rocking gently in the lapping surf. My father was a quiet man, like my grandfather, who was slow to speak. When Grandfather did, it was almost always in Aleut. Many of the elders spoke in Aleut. I understood some of what they said, as did Mother and Father, but I spoke mostly English. That's all they taught us in school. "English Only!" teachers yelled if we spoke Aleut in class. They even punished us. One time, when I was nine, my teacher paddled me and made me stay after school because I accidentally said something in Aleut. I don't remember what I said, but it wasn't a bad word or anything.

"Untie the rope and help me drag the seal up the beach," said my father.

The seal was heavy, but I was glad to help. I tugged

with all my might, and together we dragged the seal up to a drift-log above the high-tide line. Because there are no trees for a thousand miles, the log had drifted on the sea from just about anywhere before being washed ashore on our island. In truth, I don't think Father needed my help at all. Girls aren't allowed to hunt, but I wanted to be a great hunter like my father, who was the best one in our village. He almost always returned with a seal or a sea lion, which he shared with elders who were too old to hunt any longer and who had no sons to hunt for them.

Father was always teaching me the proper way to act.

Many times he told me, "When a hunter is lucky enough to get a seal he must share it with those who are not so lucky. When the seal's spirit sees the hunter's generosity and how he used every part, wasting nothing, it will tell its kin to give themselves to that man in the future because they know he is respectful. Someday, Kiska, you will be old or sick and depend on others to help you. That's our way. That's always been our way. You remember that. A great chief is someone who provides for the people and takes care of them."

"When I grow up, I want to be a hunter," I said proudly, yet knowing my father's response.

"How many times have I told you that girls aren't allowed to hunt or fish? They aren't even allowed to touch a kayak. It brings bad luck. They can pick berries and gather seagull eggs and clams; they can cut and dry salmon and other fish and render seal oil, but men do the hunting and fishing."

"Well, I don't think it's fair," I grumbled, crossing my arms across my chest. "Someday I'm going to be a hunter, and I'm going to help our people. You'll see."

I was quiet after my father gave me a scolding look.

I sat on the massive gray log and watched as he skinned the seal. My older sister, Donia, came out from the house and sat beside me, holding her chubby three-month-old baby girl named Mary. Even though Donia was only nineteen years old, she was already a widow. Her husband disappeared a month before Mary was born. He had gone out seal hunting alone. A sudden winter storm blew in from Siberia and her husband never returned. Day after day, Donia walked up the footpath and stood at the edge of the highest cliff holding her baby in her arms looking out over the dark sea, hoping to catch a glimpse of her husband. In her grief, she imagined every whitecap on the horizon was a kayak. She went up there every day for almost two months. She didn't eat, and her baby started to go hungry for milk. Mother sent me up every afternoon with a pail of food for my sister. I sat beside her and watched the swelling sea, encouraging her to eat for her baby's sake.

But Donia didn't want to eat. She didn't want to live. I was afraid that she would jump off the cliff with her baby.

"But you have to go on for Mary's sake," I said. "Mary is half you and half her father. He still lives in her. Look at her. Can't you see his face in hers?"

I think what I said affected Donia. After that, she stopped going up to the cliff and took better care of herself and Mary.

Uncle had also got a seal, and he dragged it up beside my father's seal. Together they skinned the seals and cut up the meat while my sister and I and little Mary watched.

"Fur seals and sea otters and sea lions are very important to our way of life," said my uncle. "We make our kayaks from their tanned skins. We stay warm from their fur and dry from waterproof raincoats made from their skin. Their meat makes us healthy and strong. From their fat we make oil, which we use for many things."

"Tell the story of the first seals," I pleaded excitedly, although I had heard it many times.

"What did I tell you about the proper way to ask for things?" my father said sternly.

"Please, Uncle," I said in a calmer tone. "Please tell me the story."

Father nodded that I had done right.

Uncle told us the story while skinning his seal, careful to keep his mind on his work.

"A very long time ago, there were no seals in the sea. There were fish and seabirds and whales, but there were no seals. Back then, there was a village on one of the other islands. In that village a young girl had just turned of marrying age. She was very beautiful. Every young man wanted to marry her. One night, a man crept into her room while she was asleep and forced himself on her. It was so dark that the girl couldn't see who it was. All the same, she fought back, but she was not as strong as the man. This went on for several nights. Then that girl thought of a plan. The next time the man came for her, she would scratch his face so as to mark him. Sure enough the man returned under darkness, and true to her plan, the girl scratched his face. The next day, she walked around the village looking for a man with a scratch on his face. To her horror, the man turned out to be her older brother. In her great shame, the girl ran to the cliffs and threw herself into the sea. But instead of drowning, she came up as a seal—the very first female seal. Because the brother loved his sister so much, or maybe because he was ashamed of what he had done, the brother also jumped off the cliff, coming up as the first male seal. All seals thereafter came from the two of them."

For a while I sat in silence, thinking about the story. Although I had heard it many times, I was always uncomfortable with the ending. It seemed to me that the wicked brother got his desire to be with his sister. I had heard another version in which the incestuous brother and sister become the first sea otters. What was to be learned from such stories? That life is unfair? Our stories weren't like the fairy tales I heard at school with their tidy, happy endings.

Suddenly, we heard rumbling in the distance. Father and Uncle stood up from their work, stretched, turned eastward, and listened. The rumbling seemed to go on for several minutes.

"Sounds like thunder coming from Dutch Harbor," Father said, matter-of-factly. "A storm's coming. Better get ready for it."

My grandmother, who I called Umma, came down to the beach carrying an empty pail, which Father and Uncle filled with chunks of meat. We used almost every part of a seal or sea lion, including the flippers from which we made "stink flipper," a delicacy made by letting the flippers ferment in a container buried in the ground for a long time. My grandmother and other elders love it. I can't stand the smell of it. You can die from eating it if it's prepared improperly.

"Kiska," my father said to me. "Help your grandmother."

"Here, Umma," I said, sliding off the gray log and grabbing the pail handle. "Let me carry this for you."

Grandmother smiled and patted me on the head.

"You a good granddaughter," she said.

My grandfather died last year. I called him Uppa. He caught a bad cold during the winter, which eventually turned into pneumonia. Mother said it had to do with water in his lungs. I said why don't we hold him upside down and let the water spill out, that way he'd get better. Mother laughed at me and smiled sadly. They took Uppa on a boat to a hospital far away, where he died a week later. Grandmother has been sad ever since then. They were married for over forty years.

I wanted to go look for more eggs on the cliffs when I was done carrying the pail for Umma, but Mother put me to work as soon as we walked into the house.

"Empty the honey bucket and sweep the floor when you get back."

It was usually my older brother's chore to empty

the bucket, but Peter was out seal hunting by himself. Mother didn't like that he went out on the sea all alone. But at seventeen, Peter was a loner with a rebellious streak a mile long. Father comforted Mother by reminding her that he and his brother had learned to hunt by themselves when they were about Peter's age. With my brother gone, it fell to me to empty the smelly bucket.

"Yes, Mother," I said grudgingly.

She was always coming up with chores for me to do, said it kept me out of trouble.

I hated emptying the smelly bucket, which sloshed as I carried it with both hands on the wire handle to the far edge of the village, where I poured it into a deep hole that was used by the community for such a purpose. When I returned, I swept the floor and then mother had me chop up potatoes for the seal soup she was cooking for dinner. Potatoes are pretty much the only vegetable that grows on our sunless island where there is little difference between summer and winter. No matter the season, we can count on rain, wind, clouds, and fog more than three hundred days a year. It may seem harsh to you, but it's the only world we know.

It's beautiful in its own way.

During our dinner of boiled seal and potatoes with hard bread, Father kept looking out the window, anxiously searching the horizon for approaching thunder clouds. Although it was cloudy as usual, patches of blue sky shone through spaces between clouds.

"Looks like the storm is going to miss us," he said with a relieved smile.

After dinner we all went to church for evening prayers. Our church is beautiful. The outside is painted white with blue trim around the windows and doors and the roofline and a tall golden Russian Orthodox cross projects into the gray sky above the blue, crown-shaped steeple. Every summer the people of our village repaint the outside of the church so that it is always sparkling white. Every Easter we celebrate with a procession in which respected men carry large crosses and we all sing hymns as we parade through our village and up the grassy footpath to the cliffs above our village, where the priest blesses our village. Then we parade back down to the beach where he blesses the sea and prays for every seal hunter's safe return.

Behind the church is a small cemetery with the graves of our people. Little houses, about six feet long and three feet high, sit atop every grave enclosed by a short, white picket fence. These are the houses for the souls of the dead. My grandfather is buried there, as are all my relatives from the past.

The inside of our church is even more beautiful than the outside. Wonderfully painted and gilded icons from Russia with images of Christ and Mary with the infant Jesus adorn the white walls. One window is made of stained glass. Polished brass censors and candlesticks with long white candles embellish the nave where the priest delivers Mass.

Our church is the pride and joy of our community, the center of our lives. Everyone goes to church and everyone takes care of it. Every two weeks, Mother and

Umma scrub the floor, while Father and Uncle clean the windows, inside and out. My uncle's wife, who I call Auntie, dusts all the pictures and crosses on the walls. My job is to polish the brass until I can see my face in it.

Because our villages are so small and the Aleutian Chain is so long—more than a thousand miles—a traveling priest visits by boat only a few times a year, making his rounds from village to village, east to west, down the Chain and then back up again. A layman from our village helps in between.

I know what you're thinking. What does our little village have to do with Russia?

In school, we learned that Alaska used to be owned by Russia. They came here for the fur seals and the sea otters. Over a hundred years and longer, the Russians killed millions of them for their rich fur, almost slaughtering them to extinction. Back then, the Russians treated my people terribly. They killed many Aleuts and enslaved entire villages to catch seals for them. Many Aleuts died from diseases the Russians brought to our islands. Like the seals and otters, they almost wiped us off the face of the earth. Russia eventually sold Alaska to the United States in 1867. Alaska is not yet a state, but we hope it will be one day. The men in our village talk about it often.

The only good thing the Russians left us was our beloved Russian Orthodox Church, the center of our village life. That, and our last names, all of which are Russian.

Mine is Baranoff.

Some elders still believe in the old ways, the way we did before the Russians came with their guns and their diseases and their bibles. They tell stories of how Raven made the world, including the sea, our islands, and even us Aleuts. Our priest tells us that those old stories, like the one about the first seals, are just superstition. He says they are bad, but I don't see anything wrong with telling them. It's part of who we are. Besides, I like them.

When we came home from our evening service, Father turned on the radio and the entire family sat around it and listened, the way we did every night. I sat on an empty kerosene tin turned upside down cradling Mary in my arms, rocking her gently to help her fall asleep while Donia washed dirty diapers in a bucket, wringing them out by hand to hang and dry on a line outside. Winston, our dog named after Winston Churchill, was curled up asleep at my feet, his legs occasionally fluttering and kicking as if running in a dream, chasing sea gulls, no doubt. When Mary finally closed her eyes, I gestured for Donia to look. She leaned over and studied her little girl's peaceful face and smiled. Often when Mary is asleep, I notice how much she looks a little like me because her mother is my sister and we look so much alike. The snappy band music we were listening to was suddenly interrupted by a broadcaster's urgent and breathy announcement:

"This morning, and again this afternoon, Japanese aircraft launched from two Imperial Japanese light carriers raided and bombed Dutch Harbor Naval Base and nearby Fort Mears in the Aleutian Islands of western Alaska. Seventy-eight Americans were killed and fourteen aircraft and the transport ship, *Northwestern*, were destroyed. Two barracks and the radio station were also destroyed. American anti-aircraft gunners shot down two Jap dive bombers and a fighter plane during the short-lived battle. Three more Zeroes were shot down in aerial dogfights over the Pacific on their return to the carriers. Repeat. The Japanese have attacked Alaska."

CHAPTER 2
Evacuation

During the following days and weeks, airplanes as silvery as salmon flew overhead on their way to and from the end of the long chain of islands. Sometimes we counted as many as eight flying in formation like a flock of geese. From the cliff tops we could see gray warships on the horizon steaming westward. The news on the radio was that the Japanese had invaded two islands at the end of the Aleutian Chain. My mother once told me that she had named me after one of the islands.

We celebrated my fourteenth birthday with a cake and candles and presents.

Everyone in the village was talking about the war and whether or not the Japanese would continue their invasion eastward along the chain toward the mainland, toward our village. Some of the men took to standing on the cliff tops with their hunting rifles slung over their shoulders while watching for Japanese ships through binoculars. A few even dug holes in the hillsides above the beachhead. Uncle said they were called fox holes, but I thought they looked more like empty graves.

The whole idea of war frightened me. I couldn't imagine our peaceful lives on our beautiful island being shattered by war.

One day a gray ship with an American flag arrived and anchored offshore where the water was deep. Three smaller boats were lowered from the ship, and we watched as men clambered into them and headed for our village. Everyone ran down to the beach to greet them. Village dogs stood at the water's edge barking at the approaching crafts, but they settled down when they saw it was only men in boats, a common sight in a seaside village.

When the boats landed at our beach, men in Army uniforms jumped out. Several of the men had rifles. The oldest—a tall, thin man with little silver eagles on the shoulders of his uniform and on his hat and with a holstered pistol on his belt—ordered that everyone from our village come down to the beach to hear what he had to say. Several boys ran up the rocky path to the village to spread the word. Within minutes, everyone—young and old alike—were standing on the beach anxious to hear what the pistol-wearing man had to tell them.

"Is this everyone?" he asked one of the older men from our village.

"Yes," replied the man after looking around at the anxious faces. "We are all here."

In the excitement, he hadn't noticed that my brother was not in the crowd. Peter hadn't returned from his hunting trip.

The officer lit a cigarette, pulled out a piece of paper from his shirt pocket, unfolded it, and read it aloud, carefully exaggerating every word:

• • • •

By order of the Secretary of the United States War Department and by the Secretary of the Interior, you are hereby ordered to abandon your village immediately and to be relocated to a safer location where you will be interned for the duration of the war against the Japanese. Such orders are in the interest and security of the nation and for your own protection.

• • • •

Many questions followed.

"Where are we to go?" asked one man.

"Why can't we stay here?" asked another.

"What does *interned* mean?" asked my mother.

The officer told us that we were to leave immediately, at that very minute with only what we had on. No one was permitted to go home to collect clothes or pots and pans, or to close house doors or windows. No one was allowed to leave the beach. He ordered us to board the three boats immediately, to be transferred to the gray ship anchored a couple hundred yards offshore. When several families disregarded the orders and started up the path to their homes, two soldiers ran in front of them and aimed their rifles at them. Suddenly everyone was shouting and talking. Many people were crying. Young children clung to their parents. The man with the silver eagles raised his pistol into the air and shot at the clouds.

I could hear the echo of the blast off the cliffs behind me. My ears rang.

The commotion stopped.

"You must come with us now!" he yelled, flicking his cigarette on the beach and waving his pistol.

"But why must we go now?" asked my father. "Why can't we first gather some belongings to take with us?"

Someone in the back of the crowd shouted, "We're American citizens! We have rights!"

I think it was Donia.

"I have my orders," replied the officer sternly. "But I can tell you it's for your own good. The Japanese have already taken two islands west of here. They may be heading this way. We don't want you people to be harmed or captured. Besides, some fighting may take place in this area and . . . well . . . you all kind of look like Japs to us. We wouldn't want to accidentally shoot some of you in the heat of battle."

At gun point they loaded us into the boats and ferried us to the waiting transport ship. I remember on the side of the ship was painted the name, *Delarof*. As we boarded, a short, bald man with a clipboard asked us our names, which he wrote down, often asking first how to spell them.

"Name?" he asked me when it was my turn.

"Kiska."

"Last name," he grumbled.

"Baranoff."

"Age?"

"Fourteen," I answered proudly.

The man didn't even look at me. He just told me to move along.

"Name?" I heard him say to the next person in line as he methodically inventoried the human cargo.

After the last of our people were aboard, counted, and our names all written down in the list, we were sent down into the hold of the ship. It was cold and dark, but there were small round windows through which we could see our village. Already in the hold were Aleuts from a village on a nearby island. We were related to some of the families.

Mother and Father spoke to some of them. They said the same thing had happened to them. The ship had arrived and soldiers had come ashore and ordered them to board the ship immediately. They told us how the soldiers had killed all their pets and used kerosene to set their village on fire after they were all aboard. They watched in dismay as their village and church burned to the ground. Everything they owned, including their kayaks, was consumed in the flames. The people wept on retelling the story of what had happened to them and to their homes.

Suddenly, we heard gunfire from outside. Thinking a battle with the Japanese was underway we ran to the tiny windows and looked out. Soldiers with rifles were walking through our village and in and out of our homes shooting our pet cats and dogs. I watched one soldier shoot a cat sitting on an empty fuel drum. I saw my dog running up the path to the cliffs above our village, trying to escape. A soldier ran after him, shooting at him and missing him several times. Rocks and dirt flew up where the bullets struck too high or too low. But finally, the soldier knelt and aimed right and killed my dog. I can still see him rolling and rolling down the hill and lying in a clump of grass.

I'll probably see him like that for the rest of my life.

Later, we were told that the soldiers had killed our pets for their own good, so that they wouldn't starve to death or suffer in the abandoned village. They said we would be gone for a long time, but no one told us for how long.

No one really told us much of anything.

After that, the ship weighed anchor and steamed eastward. As I lost sight of my village and our church, I wondered if I'd ever see them again. Over the next week or longer, we stopped at seven more Aleut villages, including St. George and St. Paul on the Pribilof Islands, which are far north of the other islands. From the windows we saw the familiar scene played out over and over. The colonel—we were told that was his rank—went ashore with soldiers in boats to read the government order to the villagers. Once the confused and frightened people were aboard and properly accounted for, soldiers killed their dogs and cats. Of the seven villages where we stopped, two were burned to the ground. The colonel told us he had to do that. He said that certain villages had strategic value. But other villages, he said, were not as important and so they were burned so the Japanese would not be able to use them or anything in them if they invaded this far up the Aleutians.

In all, there were 881 of us from nine different villages crowded into the ship's dingy hold. The list of family names was long: Merculief, Shelikoff, Ermeloff, Galovin, Kenezuroff, Snigaroff, Andreanoff, Krukof, Kuzakin, Nevzuroff, Gromoff, Tutiakoff, Tutrakoff, Kochutin, Philemenoff, Ermeloff, Berikoff, Kudrin, Yakmenoff, Zacharof, Sumarokoff, Nikoloff, Borenin, Bourukofsky, Shabolin, Shangin, Lekankoff, Petrivelli, Dushkin, Lestenkof, Gustigoff, Prokopiof, Sovoroff, Horoshoff, Golodova, Suvoroff . . .

I hope I haven't forgotten any names. It's been such a long time.

And, of course, there was my family: the Baranoffs.

Everyone in my family, that is, but Peter. Mother was concerned about what would happen to him when he returned to our village and found everyone gone.

"Don't worry about Peter," said Father. "He is resourceful. He can take care of himself."

The hold was dank and dark. There were no beds for us. Each person was given a coarse green Army blanket, but the blankets did not keep us warm on the cold metal floor that always seemed damp and sucked all the warmth from our bodies. We were given only one meal a day, and we were never allowed to leave the hold. Almost nine hundred people had to use one small bathroom that ran out of toilet paper on the first day and backed up onto the floor. The hold smelled terrible. Many people vomited from the smell and from the constant rolling motion of the ship, which only made the stench worse.

We used blankets to clean the vomit.

And always—always—there was the lingering smell of diesel exhaust from the engine room.

Several babies and old folks got real sick. They called it ship's cough. Mary was one of them. She was coughing all the time and she wouldn't drink Donia's milk. She sounded like she couldn't breathe, wheezing in short desperate breaths. She looked so pale, and she hardly ever opened her eyes. Some of the village leaders asked for the ship's medical doctor to come down to help. But he didn't come. They pleaded. Still he didn't come. Father grew increasingly angry. Desperate to help his little granddaughter, he grabbed a soldier roughly and demanded that he fetch the ship doctor, but we were told the doctor wouldn't come down to the hold and that they wouldn't send the sick up to see him.

"Why doesn't the doctor come down here to help Mary and all the others?" I asked Mother. "Isn't that what doctors are supposed to do?"

Mother didn't say a word. She just looked at me sadly and kissed me on the top of my head.

After that there was a lot of praying. You could hear people softly praying at all times of the day above the constant coughing and crying—people praying for help and asking why this was happening to us and why we were being treated so badly. By chance, one man had a small bible in his coat pocket when the soldiers came. A dozen men and women huddled around him while he read from it.

There is a saying in our language: *Txin itugnigalix, chuqaa chxadax*. It means, "He who is to have much sorrow, his throat feels full."

We all felt as if we were choking.

There was nothing to do in the belly of the ship. The days dragged and the sleepless nights were filled with coughing and crying and people retching in the darkness. I made friends with a couple girls from another village who were about my age, but there was nothing to do but talk about our circumstance and to walk from one end of the hold to the other, stepping over or around people sleeping or trying to sleep. I was cold and hungry most the time and tired for lack of good sleep.

Hunger, boredom, and sickness weren't the only things with us in the hold.

Mary was the first to die. Donia held her all through the night and the morning and the next day, rocking her in her arms while weeping and whispering to her. She wouldn't give up her dead daughter until soldiers pried Mary from her arms, hurriedly wrapped her in a green blanket, and took her away. We later heard from a soldier that they had tossed her tiny body overboard into the frigid sea.

CHAPTER 3
Funter Bay

For the first time in almost two thousand miles we emerged from the reeking hold and into the blinding sunlight, where screeching seagulls hovered above the ship. About three hundred of us, my family included, were ordered off the ship. With our hands shading our eyes and the strong helping the weak, we shambled down a grated metal ramp and milled about on the long wooden dock. Most of the folks in our group were from the Pribilof Islands.

"Why us?" I wondered.

"Where are we?" a man in front of me asked a young soldier.

"Admiralty Island," came the sharp reply.

"Move along!" another soldier yelled at the dazed and milling crowd.

When no one moved, the soldier shoved a mother holding her two-year-old son.

"Move!" he shouted.

An old man standing nearby grabbed the soldier by

the arm and wheeled him around so that he faced him, looking him in the eye.

"Leave them be," the old man growled.

His glare was fierce, like a dangerous animal. The soldier, a skinny young man who couldn't have been more than twenty, backed away from the vicious glower.

"Into the woods, please," he said to the people around him without shouting. "Down the trail."

Everyone began to shuffle toward the end of the dock. I looked back and saw the old man hobbling along near the end of the forming line. As we trudged across the creaking dock we took in the towering landscape before us.

Trees all crammed together grew to unbelievable heights with vine-strangled trunks so wide that it would take several people holding hands to reach around one. No sunlight penetrated the teeming boughs. Moss clung to the trunks like shaggy fur, and ferns and other plants engulfed the earth itself. Low clouds were snagged in the teeth of the tree tops. Some clouds seemed to have torn loose and drifted wounded until they were again raked and snared. The forest was dense and dark and unlike anything we had ever seen.

We clung to each other in fear.

I recall feeling a little ashamed that I held my mother's hand as we were pressed into the smothering darkness. I thought of myself as nearly grown. As we ambled along, closely packed, our eyes darting, I couldn't help but wonder why we were being sent into the wilderness. What would become of all the other people still inside the stifling hold?

We followed an overgrown trail that led to an old, large building that looked as though it would topple over at any minute. There were no doors and the windows were all broken. There were holes in the walls, and from where we stood we could see holes in the roof. Someone said it used to be a salmon cannery. We were told to go inside, that it was to be our quarters for the duration of the war. With only the clothes on our backs and a few carried belongings, and in need of bathing, we reluctantly entered our new home. Sunlight streamed in from the holes in the roof, casting dappled patches of light on the mossy wooden floor, which creaked as we shuffled across its splintered surface. As we made our way, exploring our new home, families staying close together, I was struck by the thick, damp odor. Plants grew in the sunbeams, moss grew in shadows, and vines crept in through the broken windows, clutching the walls, trying to pull them down. The ceiling was high, and the rafters and support beams were covered with spider webs. The walls were skeletal, the gray supporting studs visible. Shattered glass littered the dusty floors, and it looked as if animals had been living in corners of the abandoned building. Several people broke through the rotten floorboards up to their waist and had to be pulled out. It looked as though not a single human being had stepped foot inside the cannery for a hundred years.

I couldn't help but wonder if the government had even sent anyone here to investigate before delivering us here to live in such decrepitude. Did the colonel on the ship know where he was taking us? And if they did know, if they had seen the appalling state of the cannery, why didn't they find a better place for us to live? Would they bring their *own* families to live here even for a single day?

"Is *this* where we are going to live?" I asked Mother, tugging on her long, blue dress.

"I don't know," she replied softly, looking around in disbelief. "I think so, Little One."

That's what she called me sometimes. Even though I was older now, I liked the way she said it.

"But there are no beds," I complained. "Where do we sleep?

"I don't know."

"There are no tables or chairs. Where do we eat?"

"I don't know."

I started to ask another question but Mother stopped me.

"Enough questions for now. I have no answers to give you."

I tried not to cry, but looking around the empty room full of dust and glass and spider webs, I couldn't hold back.

"I want to go home," I wept. And I felt ashamed.

"I'm sorry, Kiska," she whispered. "I don't think they're going to let us go home for a while. We have to make the best of it."

Father rubbed my back reassuringly, the way he did when I was a little girl and couldn't fall asleep.

"Be strong, Daughter," he said with a weak smile that was meant to comfort me but didn't.

Donia came over and leaned against Father, her head on his shoulder. All four of us held each other. I guess knowing that my family was with me helped a bit. But I was still scared. I missed our little house in the village. I missed my little niece. I worried about my brother.

At supper time, soldiers carried in large pots of soup and bread. The soup was mostly broth with some cabbage and onions and a few carrots added. We had eaten it several days in a row on the ship. We were already sick of it. We longed for seal and dried fish and seal oil to dip the fish in. That was my favorite.

• • • •

The first night in the cannery was horrific. We all slept on the floor wrapped in our scratchy blankets. Although the days were warm enough, the nights were cold. We had no lights or candles, so everyone went to bed as soon as it was dark. Families huddled in knots for warmth. As always, the darkness was full of coughs, whimpers, snoring, and hushed conversations. There was no toilet. People just went outside close to the building to do their business because they were too afraid to walk into the forbidding woods. By morning, the weedy area along the outside walls of the cannery was disgusting with piles of feces, and smudgy prints crisscrossed the wooden planks from where people had stepped in the messes in the dark and returned to their sleeping places, the floorboards creaking as they crept about in soiled shoes.

The next day was as terrible as the night before.

Certainly, we were glad to be off the ship, but our new prison was little better than the wretched hold. Although the soldiers never said we were prisoners, we felt as if we were. They told us what to do, where to go, and most importantly, they would not let us return home to our villages.

Everyone understood that we couldn't keep using the side of the building for a bathroom, so my father and uncle found pieces of old scrap lumber beneath the building and fashioned a makeshift toilet at the edge of the clearing near the small creek. It was little more than a rickety wall to crouch behind and a shallow hole they had dug with their hands and sticks. Without toilet paper, we had to use leaves or fistfuls of grass or weeds. Moss worked, too.

Another group of men and women went about picking up the mess from the night before, using sticks or leaves to collect the many piles. The entire time the soldiers assigned to watch us stood by doing nothing, smoking cigarettes and telling jokes. I think many of the jokes were about us. I didn't like the way they looked at some of the older girls. Father said he had overheard that the other Aleuts on the ship had been sent to nearby internment camps, similar to ours. He said he had heard that each camp could only house about two hundred of us.

We asked the soldiers for more blankets and some twine. They returned with stacks of the rough, green blankets and spools of brown twine. Families used the twine and blankets to partition the cannery into smaller living spaces, hanging the blankets to create privacy walls. As many as eight people or more shared spaces only less than ten feet squared.

Donia sat alone for the most part, staring blankly at nothing or sobbing into her hands. She didn't help out with the chores of making the cannery livable, but everyone understood. They all knew what had happened on the ship. At such a young age, Donia had lost her entire little family in the span of only a few months. A heart can take only so much loss. Without Mary, nothing remained to remind Donia of her husband. I could see the black gloom engulfing her, a shroud as ominous as clouds ensnared in the giant trees. I suspected, were we home, my sister might throw herself off a cliff into the sea.

I didn't know what to say to my sister, so I avoided her.

CHAPTER 4
Home Bitter Home

If there was one thing that Funter Bay had in common with home, it was the rain. The rain and the impenetrable fog that made everything wet. It rained almost every day, pouring through the holes in the roof, and blasting through the broken windows and gaping doorways. There were few dry places to huddle. We were wet and cold and miserable most of the time. A lot of people, mostly elders, got sick. We hung the sopping blankets out to dry in the daytime whenever the rain stopped, but the sky was almost always cloudy, so it took most the day for the blankets to dry, if they did at all.

Although it was summer, I recall very few sunny days.

After a while, the blankets smelled moldy. It didn't help that none of our clothes had been washed since leaving our villages. The cannery began to smell of mildew and waste and body odor. The stench permeated the decaying wood and planks. Some of my most vivid memories of those first days are of the smells.

Eventually, after almost a month, a council of elders complained to Mr. Anderson about the appalling conditions of the cannery. Mr. Anderson was our camp superintendent. He was a tall man with a tight paunch for a belly, a sallow, thin face with a hawk nose. His beige uniform always looked as if it had been freshly starched and ironed and he always wore his hat cocked askew. He always seemed anxious, speaking too fast, and he always had a corn cob pipe in his mouth.

Some people joked that he was trying to be like General MacArthur.

While we lived in the drafty, ramshackle cannery, he and the guards lived in a house. It had fresh white paint and a door and unbroken windows with light blue curtains. The shingled roof kept the inside dry, and wood smoke wafted from a chimney pipe in the cool, wet evenings and nights. Brightly colored flowers grew in window boxes. I looked inside once from the doorway, and I could see neatly arranged furniture and bunk beds. There was a white vase of purple and yellow flowers on the round kitchen table, and the smell of fresh coffee drifted out the open door. I could hear music from a radio. They even had electric lights and a generator. Every few days, a boat from Juneau delivered fresh meat and vegetables and cases of beer for the Keepers. That's what we called Mr. Anderson and his staff of guards. While our jailors had steak and ham and pork chops, we begged for the bones to boil broth.

After the council complained, we received promises that things would be made better. Mr. Anderson listened attentively and made a list of the things we asked for as he puffed his pipe.

Two weeks later, a small supply ship arrived with hammers, nails, saws, axes, window panes, lumber, tar paper and shingles for the roof, ladders, cans of paint and paint brushes, cots, more blankets, pots, pans, and plates and bowls . . . everything we needed to make the place livable. And waterproof. There were large cans of food and heavy sacks of flour and washboards and lye soap for washing our clothes. There was even a wood stove made from an empty fifty-gallon fuel drum.

Everyone cheered when we saw the cases of toilet paper.

Over the following days and weeks, we repaired the cannery while soldiers sat around idly playing cards or dice, gambling with money or cigarettes, and whistling at the young women who walked past them, including Donia. Several men built a proper outhouse at the end of the long dock. It even had a door. The outhouse had two holes, side by side. The men joked that it was so you could sit with a friend and encourage one another. They said they had thought about building a two-story outhouse, but they laughingly said that no one would use the downstairs seat. Situated at the end of the dock, the hole was essentially bottomless; waste simply fell into the sea.

It didn't take long to see the plan's error. Rolling waves and changing tides washed the waste ashore onto the pebbly beach. From the daily use of over two hundred people, the beach for a hundred yards in both directions was soon fouled. The stench and the flies were horrible. At first some of the children played on the beach, skipping stones and looking for seashells and starfish. But after a week, even they stopped playing anywhere near the dock.

The outhouse wasn't our only concern.

We learned firsthand that Admiralty Island had one of the highest concentrations of brown bears in Alaska, some weighing as much as fifteen hundred pounds. We could hear them at night sometimes, snuffling around the cannery, overturning things. One morning, we discovered paw prints on the outside wall where a bear stood to look inside a window. The muddy prints were ten feet off the ground! After that, a lot of people were afraid to go outside.

One bear brazenly stalked people on the path to the outhouse. After a few close calls, the Keepers shot him. We all got to see him up close, which terrified us all the more. His claws were as long as knives, his yellowish teeth daunting. There was nothing so ferocious or monstrous on our islands. The Keepers didn't need to build a fence to keep us from running away. The knowledge that so many bears roamed the island kept us close to the cannery.

During those first weeks, Mother continued to worry about Peter, and Father continued to reassure her as best he could.

"I'm certain Peter's okay," he'd say. "I'm sure he's living in our house just waiting for everyone to return. He's probably cooking a pot of seal meat right now."

The notion of her son cooking at her stove cheered my mother.

"In some ways, I'm glad he's there and not here," she replied.

I felt the same way. I wish I was home.

Because we had only the clothes on our backs, it didn't take long for our clothes to start falling apart. Wearing the same thing day after day is hard on seams and buttons and fabric. Knees were worn out on pants, buttons were missing, and our socks or stockings had holes. We'd all be naked if we didn't get more clothes soon. The elder committee complained again to Mr. Anderson. A week later, a fishing boat arrived to deliver boxes and boxes of used clothes. The churches in a nearby fishing town had arranged a used clothes drive to help out. There were clothes of every style and size: clothes for toddlers, children, teens, and men and women. There were clothes for big people and tall people. There were even shoes and boots. Everyone picked through the boxes, taking what they thought might fit them or their families. There was even a box of assorted buttons and needles and thread for mending.

I was helping my father and uncle, who were nailing shingles on the roof. I had also helped out the day before when they put down the thick, black tar paper that goes beneath the shingles. It was my job to wait on the ground and to fill a small gray bucket that they lowered on a white rope whenever they needed more roofing nails. I filled the bucket from a heavy box of nails sitting on the ground about midway along the cannery wall. Sometimes they yelled down for a sandwich or for some water to drink. There was a boy about my age doing the same thing at the other end of the wall. One time we met at the nail box to fill our buckets.

"I've seen you around," he said.

"That's not hard to do here," I joked.

"My name is Alexander, but my folks call me Sasha."

"I'm Kiska."

"I know. Isn't that the name of an island?"

"Yeah. My mom named me after it."

"I like it. It suits you."

"How so?"

"It's pretty . . . like you. How old are you?"

"Fourteen. How old are you?" I asked somewhat shyly.

"Fifteen."

"I saw you get on the ship when we stopped at your village," I said.

"Yeah. But there's not a village there anymore. They burned everything, even our church," Sasha said sadly. "There's nothing left for us to go home to, even if we could leave here."

I remember looking out the small round window of the hold and seeing his village on fire after everyone had boarded the ship. I was glad that the soldiers hadn't burned my village. At least my family had a home to return to . . . someday. The thought of our little house and our beautiful church waiting for us just as we had left them was heartening. I felt bad that Sasha's village was gone. I wanted to tell him how sorry I was.

"They killed my dog," was all I managed to say.

"Yeah . . . they killed mine, too. His name was Rolly."

"Mine was Winston," I replied.

Neither of us spoke for a moment. We were both recalling the awful memories of that day the ship arrived to take us away. I was trying to push away the memory of Winston tumbling down the rocky path.

"Is that your dad up there?" asked Sasha, nodding in the direction of my father and uncle working on the roof.

"That's my dad in the red shirt. The other is my uncle."

"My dad's the one wearing suspenders," replied Sasha, pointing to his father working with several other men on the other end of the roof."

Just then my father shouted down to us.

"Hey down there! Hurry up with those nails! What's taking so long?"

"I gotta get back to work. See you," I said looking over my shoulder as I carried the full bucket back to where the end of the rope lay loosely on the ground.

After tying a knot around the wire handle I yelled up to my father.

"You can pull it up now!"

For the rest of the day Sasha and I spoke whenever we could, and we smiled and waved at each other from afar when we couldn't.

While my father and uncle and the other men—Sasha's father included—worked on the roof, others built long dining tables with bench seats that could sit as many as seven or eight people on each side, picnic table style. But there was only enough lumber and plywood to build a few such tables. Of two hundred people, only about fifty could sit and eat at any one time. The rest of us had to eat standing up, sitting on the floor, or waiting for a place at the table.

All in all, the cannery was becoming livable. The roof no longer leaked. The wind and rain no longer blasted through broken windows and doors. Rotten planks on the floor were replaced. But we all missed our island homes, the cloud-tangled cliffs above our villages, the wind-riven sea, the wave-bobbing seagulls and seals, and the boundless horizon.

Most of all, we missed our beautiful church.

Eventually, we made our own church, of sorts. By luck or fate, we had the bible in camp, the one read aloud in the hold of the ship that had brought us here. One of the men made a cross from pieces of wood and painted it white. We held makeshift Masses in the cannery, trying our best to carry on the way we had been taught. It wasn't as ceremonious, and nowhere near as lovely, as our church back home, but having Mass weekly—as crude as it was and without a priest—somehow made our imprisonment more bearable. Even though we had no hymn book, we sang songs that we all knew by heart to lift our spirits—songs like "Amazing Grace" and "Onward Christian Soldiers."

Sometimes we got to read newspapers when Mr. Anderson and his staff were finished with them. The headline one day said that five thousand Japanese were building airfields and ship docks on Kiska and Attu, and that American bombers were making daily raids on the islands. The article said a Jap ship had been sunk in Kiska Harbor. It went on to say that the islands had to be recaptured because Japanese bombers launched from the Aleutians could reach Seattle, one of the most important airplane manufacturers during the war.

CHAPTER 5
Peter the Defiant

One day a small ship was reported coming into Funter Bay. Before it was even moored at the dock, word had spread that it was delivering more Aleuts to the already crowded camp. Almost everyone was waiting to see who would be joining us. But only one person was escorted off the ship. From where we stood, it looked like a man with his arms bound behind his back. Two soldiers led him down the gangway. The closest soldier shoved him roughly from behind. The captive turned and lunged at him like a wild animal, trying to head-butt him. The soldier almost fell down trying to back away.

Everyone on the dock wondered who the wild Aleut could be.

The two soldiers accompanied the man to the bottom of the gangway, where one of them untied the rope that bound his hands. As soon as his hands were free the Aleut spun around and punched one of the soldiers in the stomach. The other soldier jumped the Aleut and the two men grappled on the dock, while the sucker-punched soldier was still bent double on his knees trying to catch his breath. A third soldier ran down the metal gangway and jumped into the fray. Together, they managed to subdue the Aleut.

All of us watching marveled at the man's defiance.

I'm sure I wasn't the only person who wondered who it was.

Together, the three soldiers escorted the Aleut to where we all stood. When they were close, one of them shoved their prisoner at us.

"Good riddance," he said, as they all turned and walked back toward the ship, looking over their shoulders.

I was shocked when I saw who it was.

It was my brother, Peter.

Mother and Father pushed through the crowd and embraced their only son.

"Let me get a good look at you," said Father, holding Peter by the shoulders.

It was clear that Peter had been in a few fights. He had a few scrapes and a black eye.

"When are you ever going to learn?" said Father, shaking his head and smiling.

"I'm hungry," Peter replied.

As we all walked back to the camp, I could hear people whispering about my brother. Once inside the cannery, Father guided Peter to one of the long tables while Mother and I got Peter a bowl of soup with a large piece of stale bread.

"It's best if you dip the bread in the soup," said

Mother, hugging her son from behind and kissing him on the head.

A few people standing nearby chuckled.

Peter ate as if he were starved. Mother scolded him to slow down, but he kept on eating like a wild animal. He didn't speak until every drop of soup had been sopped up with the last piece of bread.

"They didn't feed me on the ship ever since I tried to escape three days ago," he said, wiping his mouth on his sleeve. "When we were close to land I jumped and tried to swim for shore. They locked me up after that."

Peter held up the empty bowl to me.

"Is there more?" he asked.

I refilled it from the near-empty pot on the wood stove.

"How have you been, son?" asked Father. "Why has it taken so long for them to bring you here?"

Peter waited to tell his story until after he consumed the second bowl of soup.

"I came home from hunting and found the entire village was empty. There was nobody. All the dogs and cats had been killed, even Winston," he said, looking at me to see my reaction.

"I know," was all I mustered.

"The houses were all left open. Plates and bowls with food in them were still sitting at kitchen tables beside cups of tea. It was spooky, like everyone just suddenly disappeared. I figured the Japs had come and captured everyone. I figured the only thing to do was to stay in the village, so I lived in our house. But then one day a warship arrived and all these soldiers came ashore. I saw they were American, so I went to ask a couple guys if they knew what had happened to all of you. Wouldn't you know, those numbskull soldiers starting shooting at me, yelling "Japs!" so I hightailed it out of there."

Those of us standing around remembered what the colonel had said that day on the beach.

"You all kind of look like Japs."

"For the next few weeks I lived off the land, hiding from the soldiers in the mountains. Sometimes I snuck back to the village to steal the things I needed to survive, right under their nose, you know? But they kept sending reconnaissance parties to find me. They must have really thought I was a Jap. I had some pretty close calls, but I always managed to escape. They didn't know the island like I did . . . the way you taught me, Dad."

Father placed a hand on Peter's shoulder and squeezed it firmly.

"One night they surrounded my little cave and caught me when I came out in the morning to look for food. And here I am."

"I'm just glad they didn't shoot you," said Mother, obviously relieved that her son was alive and well.

She hugged Peter.

"Me, too," I said, giving my big brother a hug around the neck.

Donia also hugged Peter. For the first time since we left our village our family was together. Everyone, that is, except Mary, who lay at the bottom of the sea.

"Where's Mary?" Peter asked Donia, looking around for his little niece.

Donia began sobbing and walked away hurriedly with her face in her hands.

• • • •

That evening, Peter and I sat against an outside wall of the cannery talking about our experiences, while I made a necklace out of dandelions for my sister.

"This place sure is a dump," he said.

"You should have seen it when we first got here," I replied. "We fixed it up pretty good."

Over the next hour, I told Peter about the day the ship arrived to take us away. I told him how we watched as they shot all of our pets. I told him how I saw one of the soldiers kill Winston. I told him how we watched later as they burned several of the villages to the ground.

As he listened, Peter's eyes narrowed and I could see him clenching his jaw.

I told my brother about our life at the cannery and about how we were treated on the ship. I told him how his niece died because the ship doctor refused to come down to the hold to help the sick. I could see that he was especially sad about Mary's death. Peter had been close to Donia's husband. Only a few years difference, they had gone hunting together many times. I saw him wipe one of his eyes with the back of a hand.

But then his pain turned back to anger.

"Listen to me, Kiska. These white people are our enemies, American or not. We're prisoners of war, make no mistake about it. We can't just sit here and take it. We can't let them do this to us. We have to fight back like . . . like the French Resistance."

"What can we do?" I asked.

"We can make their life hell, that's what we can do. We can sabotage their machines, ignore their rules and orders, disrupt their plans for us . . . make them wish they had never heard of Aleuts."

I have to say, listening to Peter talk about resistance and sabotage, I was a little worried about the trouble he might get into.

Or get me into.

CHAPTER 6
Agafon

One day while returning from the forest with an armful of firewood, I saw an old man sitting on a stump at the edge of the clearing around the cannery. He was whittling a piece of wood with a pocketknife. I recognized him as the old man who had stood up to the soldier on the dock the day we arrived. I had seen him many times around camp, always sitting and eating alone. The old man looked up and smiled at me when I walked past him. The wrinkles on his face were deep and braided, like tiny rivulets carved on a muddy tidal flat at low tide. His gray-white hair was surprising long and thick for his age, giving the impression of wildness. But his smile was warm and disarming. Grandfather used to smile at me that same way. I walked past him at first, but then I stopped and turned around.

"Hello," I said, smiling back. "What are you making?"

"Something magical," he replied, returning to his work.

"Can I see it?"

"Not yet. It not finished. Just one more thing."

He spoke the way some of the elders did, the ones who spoke mostly Aleut and struggled to speak English.

I watched as the old man bored a hole in the piece of wood with the sharp end of his pocketknife. Then he pulled a length of thin leather through the hole and tied the ends in a special knot, making the whole into a necklace.

"For you," he said, holding out the object.

"For me?" I asked, dropping my pile of firewood and taking it from his wrinkled hand.

I turned it over and over. The carving was in the likeness of a sea lion, about the size of my palm.

"It's beautiful," I said.

"I knew you would like it. I made it for you," said the old man.

"How could you have made it for me? We just met."

"All the same, I make it for you, Kiska."

He knew my name. That startled me.

"How do you know my name?"

"I know many things about you. I know what in your heart. I know what you want to become, what you *will* become . . . what you *must* become."

I said nothing as I stood there holding the carving and staring dumbfounded. I tried to hand it back, but the old man would not reclaim it.

"It yours now. It never mine."

The old man closed the thin folding blade, slid the knife into his pants pocket, and then struggled unsteadily to get up from the stump.

"It has great magic," he said as he shuffled away.

I watched him disappear into the forest. I studied the necklace again, feeling its smooth surface, its rounded edges. I even smelled it. The dark brown leather smelled of wood smoke. I pulled the necklace over my head, pulling my long hair out of the way. Then I collected the pile of firewood and carried it inside the cannery and dropped the armful into a wooden crate beside the wood stove. My father approached me, his face scrawled with a look of concern.

"I saw you talking to that old man outside. I want you to stay away from him."

"But why?" I asked. Father had never before told me to avoid another person. "He was nice."

"Just do as I say. It's for your own good," replied Father with a sternness that was unwavering. "I mean it, Kiska. Stay away from him."

"I will, Father. But can you tell me *why* so I will understand? You always taught me to respect the elders, to help them and to learn from them."

I could tell from my father's expression that he knew he had to explain his command if he wanted me to obey him.

"What do you want to know?" he asked, sitting down at one of the long tables.

"What's his name? Where does he come from?" I asked.

"They call him Agafon . . . Agafon Krukoff. But that's not the name he was born with. No one knows the name his parents give him. They say he was born before Russia sold Alaska to America. He must be at least . . . eighty, eighty-five years old," said my father, adding up numbers in his head. "But no one is certain of that either. He could be older . . . much older."

"Why doesn't anyone know his name?" I asked.

"When he was a boy, some seal hunters found him living alone on one of the islands. There was no one else alive on the whole island. They say he was like a wild animal, filthy with long, matted hair. He didn't speak a word. They say he growled and wailed like an animal when the men caught him, put him in the belly of a kayak, and brought him back to their village. He was to be raised by an old woman named Krukoff."

I tried to imagine the boy's life alone on the island without any grown-ups. What had happened to his people? How long had he been alone? How did he survive? What did he eat? I had many questions.

"Some people say he's a shaman, maybe the last one."

My interest was aroused on hearing the word *shaman*. I had heard the word only once before when my Father and uncle were talking to a priest about something. I think it was about someone who was really sick and needed help. I don't remember what they said except that the priest was angered on hearing the word and told them never to speak of it again.

"But why can't I? . . ."

"Enough," my father said sharply, glaring at me. "Just stay away from him."

Father stood up and walked away to work on some project with my uncle.

Several days later, I was washing and scouring several

large cooking pots down by the little creek that ran behind the cannery when Agafon came up and sat down beside me on the bank. I was nervous, recalling what Father had told me. I worried that he'd be angry with me if he saw me sitting with the old man. At first neither of us spoke. I just kept washing the pots, carefully watching him in the corner of my eye.

"My father told me not to talk to you," I said finally, feeling uncomfortable.

"Why you think he say that?" asked Agafon.

I told him the story Father had told me, about him being found living like a wild animal.

"Hmm," replied Agafon after listening. "There some truth to what he say, but like every story, there always more."

"Will you tell me what happened?" I asked.

Agafon adjusted his sitting position, trying to get comfortable, before beginning his story.

"When I was little boy, some Russians came to my village. I not remember how old I was, maybe five or six. A few days after they leave everyone get sick. Their bodies covered with red spots. Then people start to die. At first only a few die and we bury them. But then too many people die, and there not enough healthy people to bury the dead. Bodies lay everywhere. Whole families lay dead outside their houses. The whole village smelled of rot and death. I remember seeing dogs eat some of the bodies because their owners were dead or too sick to feed them. My folks died, my father first. My mother try to help him, but she caught the spots and died. Everyone in my village died but me. I never even get sick."

Agafon's voice trailed at the end of his story, as if he was lost in the memory.

Or trying to forget it.

"Why?" I asked. "Why didn't you get sick like the others?"

"I not know. I wonder that every day. Sometimes I feel guilty that I lived."

"What happened after that . . . after everyone died?" I asked.

"I had to keep on living. I had to eat and stay warm. That all I did—exist. That all I *could* do. I not stay in the old village for fear that the invisible death still lurked there, waiting for me."

"What did you do? Where did you go?" I asked.

"I not really remember much. Remember being hungry all time and feeling alone and scared . . . and cold. Oh yes. I remember being cold. I built a little hut from stones and sod. It not very big, just long enough to sleep in and wait out storms . . ."

I felt sad thinking how lonely he must have been, a little boy all alone on one of the most remote and barren islands in the world.

"Mostly, I remember being afraid of the dogs," he continued. "They had learned the taste of people. For a long time they try to get me. One almost did. Look here," said Agafon, pulling up his sleeve and showing me scars on his forearm. "That's where one of them got me good."

"What happened?" I asked, staring dumbfounded at the scars. I knew about dogs, of course, and I knew a little about wolves, even though there are none on our islands.

"He was my dog. He had turned wild like the others. He was part of the pack that roam the island. I had my father's harpoon and knife to fend them off. I killed him . . . my own dog. A hard thing to do, killing your own dog. They stopped coming after I kill a few of them.

"One day, after a long time—years maybe—some men come and find me. They didn't catch me at first. I knew the island better than they did. But, finally, they caught. They tie me up and put me in belly of kayak. Took me back to their village. They gave me to a woman who lived alone away from the village. She was old and never married or have children. She taught me to be human again, how to speak and how to act like a person. I learned many things from her until she died."

After that we were quiet again, until I thought of another question.

"Did you ever go back to your old village?"

"A couple times. Little by little bodies vanished, eaten by dogs and birds and animals until all that left was gray bones scattered like driftwood. It was a lonely place full of ghosts."

I thought of another question I wanted to ask.

"My father said you are a . . . a . . . shaman," I said trying to remember the word. "Are you?"

Agafon smiled.

"It nothing to be afraid of, Kiska. A shaman is some-one who know how to heal all kind of sickness, sickness of the body . . . even sickness of the spirit. He is a keeper of sacred things, mostly things long forgotten. He has special power. He can see things others cannot see, either because they cannot or will not see. Some say a shaman can see the world of the dead, which is all around us, even here, now, in this place," he said looking around at the consuming forest.

I didn't say anything at first. I was thinking about what Agafon had said about seeing the dead. I was also thinking about what he had said about my necklace being magical.

"Are *you* a shaman?" I asked slowly, although I was slightly fearful of his answer.

Agafon smiled again and got up to leave, wiping dirt from the bottom of his pants.

"I have to go now, but I can see one thing: All my life people been afraid of me. Everyone always afraid of me. They don't talk to me or be close to me. I never been married. Got no family. But you are bold and fearless. Your spirit is strong, despite your age. Our people need someone like you to help them right now. Everyone here is afraid. They don't know what to do. They feel . . . powerless," he said, struggling for the right word in English. "Their bodies are weak from meager food they give us; their spirits are weak because they no longer connected to the sea, which has always provided for us. But you, Kiska, *you* can help them."

"Me? How can I help them? What could I do? I'm

too young," I almost cried, the anxiety mounting inside me.

"You not too young. Some people have something extra added to their heart where courage and strength can grow. You one of them people."

"But I don't know what to do."

"I teach you."

"*You* could help them," I said.

"I help them by teaching *you*."

"But you could do it," I replied.

"No, I'm too old," said Agafon with sadness in his voice. "It okay to be afraid. Growing up means taking risks, and that can be fearful."

The whole idea frightened me. I frantically searched for a way out.

"What about my brother, Peter? He could do it. He's a really good hunter."

Agafon threw his head back and laughed.

"He the first person they suspect. No . . . *you* must be the one."

Having said that, Agafon left me alone by the brook side, listening to the shallow water babble like my flowing thoughts.

CHAPTER 7
Oktoberfest

The cold days and nights of October turned leaves on some trees orange and red before they fell. Those still clinging were golden in the slant afternoon sunlight. The giant, green ferns that had once swallowed the forest floor were also dying, withered and rotting into soil for next year's ferns. The forest smelled thick and sweet from fallen berries and wet and decaying wood. Our island never smelled like that in fall. From the snippets of news we overheard from the radio in the superintendent's house, we learned that the war raged on all over the world. Europe was a wasteland of crumbling and burning towns and cities with millions of people dead or fleeing to escape the ravages of the Nazis. On the other side of the world, the Pacific Ocean was a hellish sea of shipwrecks and scorched islands and charred and rotting corpses.

In the fall of 1942, it seemed as if the entire world was dying.

• • • •

One evening, Mr. Anderson announced that he was forming a work detail to make repairs on a prisoner-of-war camp for captured Germans about thirty miles away on Excursion Bay. He promised the detail would eat well. Several men asked how the Nazis came to be in Alaska, and Mr. Anderson replied that they had been captured in North Africa. They had been shipped all the way to Alaska to wait out the war. Mr. Anderson said he needed eight men and two young helpers.

"I need someone who can work on boilers and plumbing," he said turning to Sasha's father. "You're the man for it. Bring your son along if you like. He's a good worker."

Seven other men quickly raised their hands, mostly I think because of the promise of being fed well and of a getting away from camp, even if only for a day. Peter raised his hand, but Mr. Andersen said there was no way he would let him go. Although Peter hadn't been in camp for as long as the rest of us, he had already created enough trouble for the Keepers. More than once seawater had been poured into the generator's gas tank, and someone had tried to set fire to their comfortable little cottage.

Mr. Anderson suspected Peter.

I hate to say it, but I did too.

"Last thing I need is you making trouble with the Germans," he said to Peter. "Besides, you'd probably just try to escape."

He turned back to the rest of us.

"The boat leaves the dock tomorrow morning at a quarter to six, sharp," said Mr. Anderson, lighting a match and holding it just above the bowl of his pipe and taking a few long draws until the tobacco was aglow and swirling smoke obscured his face. "There will be hot coffee and breakfast aboard ship. Don't be late."

That night I couldn't sleep. I kept thinking about how the work detail was short one helper and about how much I really wanted to see what the prisoner camp looked like. But I was certain that Mr. Anderson wouldn't let a girl go. Then, an idea came to me. When I heard the detail awake in the morning, I quickly dressed in blue jeans and my father's red-and-black flannel shirt, which was far too large for me. Over that I wore a loose jacket with deep pockets, further concealing my girlness, which at fourteen wasn't all that noticeable. I shoved my long hair beneath a black woolen cap and left a note for my parents saying that I was going with the workers and not to worry. I just wanted to get away from the cannery for a day. Besides, I promised to bring back some food.

By the time they would find the note, the boat would be long gone.

• • • •

We arrived at the little cove flanking the German prisoner camp just as the sun was coming up over the surrounding mountains. As the boat approached the dock, we were astonished to see lights on the outside of the large building as well as lighted windows.

70

They had electricity!

We were ordered to disembark and to follow the skipper up a trail. As we were escorted through the building I was amazed at the condition of the place. The walls weren't stud-bare like ours. They were plastered and painted white. *And the warmth!* Although I saw no wood stove, the well-lighted building was toasty inside. As we walked down a long hallway we could hear the sound of water running and men talking on the other side of a door that was ajar. Sasha pushed open the door to look, and we saw several men taking hot showers. Two men sat on white toilets; one was reading a magazine. I looked away quickly, blushing. Sasha laughed at me. As we walked down the long hallway, I thought of our cold outhouse perched at the end of the dock.

The hallway ended in a large, high-ceilinged room with more than a dozen long tables. The number of chairs tucked up against the tables could have seated hundreds of people. Framed pictures hung on the neatly painted walls, and music was playing softly from a record player with a stack of records beside it. Books and magazines filled a long shelf built into one wall, and dozens of boxes of puzzles filled another.

We had none of the things they had.

The skipper told us to get hot coffee while he assigned our duties for the day. Sasha was assigned to help his father service the boiler in the basement and to repair some plumbing issues throughout the building. I didn't see him again until we boarded the boat late that afternoon. My chore was to paint the trim around all the doors in one hallway—about twenty, ten on each side of the hall. Each door had a number and provided entry to semiprivate rooms. As I worked my way down the hall carrying my bucket of paint, brush, and a multicolored, splattered drop cloth, I looked into the rooms. Each had two beds with clean white sheets, a wash basin, a mirror, and a dresser.

The tidy rooms reminded me of photographs I had seen of hotels.

In one room a tall man with a hairy chest and a white towel loosely wrapped around his waist was standing before the mirror shaving. He smiled and nodded as I stood in the doorway.

"Here, boy," he said in a thick accent, holding out the lather-edged razor. "You try?"

I slunk away to the next doorway, deciding that I'd go back to that one later when the man was gone.

At the end of the long wall were two rooms across from each other. Both doors were wide open. One was a barbershop. A fat German was giving a haircut and a shave to a fellow prisoner, who was reading *The Saturday Evening Post* with a Norman Rockwell picture on the cover. A radio filled with the small room with snappy music. Across the hall was a tailor's shop with two black electric sewing machines for the Germans to repair their clothing.

I don't have to tell you how upset I was seeing all this.

At noon, we were invited to take our lunch from the dining hall and to sit outside and eat. As I approached the dining hall, I could hear music and singing. A stout man was playing an accordion while the Germans sang, cheerfully hoisting foam-headed beer mugs. A colorful banner was hung across the room with the word *Oktoberfest* painted in large, bright letters. Someone told me that our lunch was at the far end of the room. As I made my way past the noisy tables, I marveled at the quantity of food. The Germans were eating some kind of enormous sausages in long pieces of bread. I later learned they are called brats, or something like that. I was appalled to see how some plates at vacated seats were still half full of food.

As I walked by a long table, one of the Germans shouted at me.

"Hey, boy! Fetch us more beer!"

I put my head down and walked faster through the noisy dining hall. From behind me I could hear laughter.

At the other end was a little store of sorts with a painted sign above an open window that read *Kantine*. I looked inside; the shelves were full of items the Germans could purchase to make their imprisonment more comfortable. Cigarettes dominated the shelves, but there was also candy and shaving soap and a hundred other items.

Our lunch consisted of thin-cut cheese and bologna. There was a plate full of pickles beside a basket full of rolls, and a jar of yellow paste with a knife sticking out of it. One of the men in our group told me it was called mustard. He said to try some on my sandwich. I quickly made six small sandwiches, sneaking five of them into my coat pockets for my family.

• • • •

That night, after we returned to Funter Bay, everyone sat at tables or on the floor or leaned against the walls or huddled around the wood stove listening as Sasha's father described what we had seen at the Nazi POW camp. He told us that he had heard that there were seven hundred Germans there. Those people not close enough to the wood stove had their blanket draped around them to stay warm. Only two flickering oil lamps lit the high-ceiling room casting skeletal shadows darkly on the stud-bare walls. Everyone was quiet and captivated as Sasha's father talked about all the conveniences and about all the food and beer . . . and about how content the Germans appeared, how they almost seemed to enjoy their imprisonment. The people gasped each time he related some comfort the Germans had but which we did not. Peter's face turned beet red. I swear I think he was about to explode from the injustice of it all.

Afterward, Sasha and I walked down to the beach and sat on a boulder beneath a starry sky listening to the lapping waves. I had a lot on my mind. And I don't know about you, but I've always found that there's nothing like a sky full of stars to put things in perspective.

"Aren't the Germans the enemy?" I asked, recalling all the news I had heard on the radio before we were forced to leave our village. "Aren't they the ones who started the war, attacking other countries and killing lots and lots of people, including American soldiers?"

Sasha didn't reply.

"Haven't they sunk hundreds, even thousands, of American ships in the Atlantic?"

Still Sasha was silent.

"I don't understand," I almost cried. "We're Americans. We haven't done anything wrong. Why is the enemy treated better than us?"

Sasha held my hand for the first time. He gently squeezed it and didn't let go.

It felt good.

We sat quietly for a long time, our fingers intertwined, while the crescent moon slid along a distant hilltop and something unseen splashed in the darkness.

When we returned to the cannery, Peter was waiting for us. He was smoking a cigarette he had stolen from one of the guards.

"I saw you two," he said in a tone I didn't like.

"So what?" replied Sasha, standing up to Peter, even though he was six inches shorter.

Peter effortlessly pushed Sasha aside.

"So, stay away from my sister," he demanded.

Then Peter turned to me.

"Guys like him only want one thing."

"I can take care of myself," I replied. "You're not the boss of me."

As Sasha and I walked away, Peter hurled one last insult at Sasha.

"Leave my sister alone. You hear me?"

. . . .

That night, I lay in my cot covered with my drab Army blanket, which barely kept me warm, even with all my clothes on and even with the wood stove rattling and popping from the fire in its belly. The nights were getting so cold that people took shifts tending the wood stove all night. Although it was still fall, we spent more and more time gathering wood during the days. I wondered how we'd make it through the coming winter. Already many people were sick. Umma was one of the sickest, coughing day and night. I also wondered about what Agafon had said, about how someone had to save the people, give them strength and hope.

Maybe he was right. Maybe Peter was also right about the need for us to fight back, to stand up for ourselves. Maybe I could help.

But how?

CHAPTER 8
My Apprenticeship Begins

The next day I found Agafon standing on the pebbly beach facing the sea, the briny wind blowing his long gray-white hair across his face. I was curious to know what he was looking at, or for what, but when I stepped close to him I saw that his eyes were closed. I stood beside him quietly, wondering if he even knew I was there. After a few minutes he opened his eyes and smiled at me. I noticed for the first time, in the bright light of day, that his left eye was clouded over and milky white.

"Good morning," he said.

"What were you doing?" I asked.

"I listening to world."

"What do you mean?"

"I *being* part of it."

I could tell by the way Agafon looked at me, at my expression, that he knew I didn't understand.

"People nowadays too busy . . . always think about what they do next. Make no time to be still. Got to live in present. See that wave?" he said, pointing to a wave just as it curled and broke and poured itself several yards up the beach, forcing a seagull to retreat to higher ground above the surf line. "It part of *this* moment and *only* this moment. That wave never come again. That seagull part of that moment too. See that cloud? It like that only right now."

Even as I looked, the wind began to rearrange the cloud's shape, pulling it apart like a cotton ball, sheering off the top, stretching it. I also noticed how its shadow had slid farther up the beach.

"We forget about nature," Agafon continued. "We think we not part of it. Just something to use. Our separation from it leaves a hole inside us, a hole filled with nothing. Most people never understand why they feel so empty. Close your eyes and listen and think of nothing else."

We stood side by side with eyes closed, feeling the sun and wind against our skin, smelling the sea and the scent of cedar and hemlock blown from the trees behind us, and listening to the sound of waves and wind and seagulls. I heard a squirrel chatter in the distance.

I broke the silence.

"The other day you told me that I could help our people. I've been thinking about that. I want to help, but I don't know what I can do to help us escape this place. But I'll try if you think I can do it."

Agafon laughed and patted my shoulder.

"I not talking about escaping, Kiska. We here 'til war over. Besides, where would we go? Our islands far away. We have no way of getting home. No, I was talking about another way to help."

I was relieved that I wasn't being asked to lead a rebellion.

"So, what can I do?" I asked.

"This place no good for our people. The food they give us weakens us more and more every day. What they feed us not good for our bodies. It keep us alive, that all. Maybe *they* want us weak. That way we no trouble. We not used to cabbage soup and white bread. We used to eating seal and sea otter, clams and mussels, fish and seal oil—*good* food from the sea, *healthy* food that make us strong. Hard to keep up spirit when stomach empty and body weak or sick."

I thought about how everyone had lost weight since June. Father had lost so much that he no longer looked powerful. Mother's face looked thin, and Grandmother looked like she might break in a strong wind. And me, too. I had to use a piece of rope to keep my pants from falling down. I also thought about all the times Father and Uncle had told me the same thing, about how the sea provides for us and takes care of us, nourishes us. I also thought about how much food the German prisoners had.

They didn't look like they were losing weight.

"But what can I do?" I asked again.

"They treat us like children here, tell us when to get up and when to go to bed. Keep eye on us all the time, even ask what we doing when we go to bathroom. Mr. Anderson and the Keepers not give weapons to our men to hunt. He afraid of what they might do. Not gonna let them go far from camp either. But you, Kiska, no one gonna notice a girl coming or going. You no danger to them. You can provide for us."

I smiled broadly, thinking about how I always told Father that I wanted to be a hunter just like him and to provide for the people. Here was my chance.

"What about the bears?" I asked, remembering the giant bear the Keepers had shot.

"You leave them alone, they leave you alone."

"Teach me," I said, making myself as straight and as tall as possible.

"There food right here in front of us," he said, waving a hand at the flat bay. "I teach you how to catch fish."

We walked back to camp—slowly, because Agafon didn't walk very fast. He didn't do anything fast. The camp tools were kept in a shed between the cannery and the cottage quartering the superintendent and his Keepers. Agafon made a few fish hooks by bending long nails with pliers into the shape of the letter "J". He sharpened the points with a file. Then he took a short length of wire and wrapped it around the shaft below the wide nail head and made a loop.

"This so you can tie a line to hook."

Agafon cut several lengths of white cotton cord—the kind used to hang laundry lines—each fifty to a hundred feet long. He tied a heavy flat washer a couple feet from the end.

"This to help line sink down deep," he said.

Then he tied a hook to the end, showing me how to make the knot. When he was done he pulled on the hook and line sharply to check that the knot held.

"Good and strong. Maybe hold big fish," he said.

Agafon showed me how to wind each hook and line carefully around a short stick to prevent tangling the lines. We placed them inside an old burlap bag with a shoulder strap.

"Now you ready to catch fish. First, you need something."

Agafon reached into his pocket and took out his pocketknife. I recognized it as the one he used to whittle my sea lion necklace.

"Fisherman need good knife. This one been mine long time," he said, as he handed it to me.

I took the knife and studied it. It was four or five inches long. The sides were made of some kind of polished gray-white wood, unlike any wood I'd ever seen. Maybe it was some kind of horn. The spine—or maybe it's called the back strap—was etched in a pattern that looked like bird wings. There's wasn't a speck of rust on the knife. It was well crafted with a good heft. I pried open the single blade.

"It good and sharp. You keep it that way," said Agafon, as he reached into his pocket and pulled out a worn sharpening stone. "I show you how."

I handed back the knife. Agafon spat on the grayish stone, turning it black, and sharpened the blade as I watched.

"You try," he said after a minute.

I spat on the stone, set the blade at the angle he showed me, and slowly, in tight circles, slid the blade across the stone.

"Not too hard . . . gently," said Agafon as he watched me. "Make sure you work whole edge up to tip. And no sharpen too much . . . make metal thin."

"Good," he said as I followed his instruction. "Now try other side like I show you."

When Agafon was sure I had learned the lesson, he checked the sharpness by cutting hairs on his wrist. Satisfied, we walked back to the beach, and Agafon showed me how to catch small fish trapped in tidal pools to use for bait. We even found one dead fish washed up on the beach.

"Put fish on hook like this," he said, showing me how so that the bait wouldn't come off easily. "Now you ready. Go way over there beyond those rocks where no one see you and fish from there. It deep there; you catch something. Bring back fish and make sure no one see you."

"Can't you come with me?" I asked.

"Them rocks hard for me to climb on. I fall and break a hip. No, I go back and sit with old women by wood stove."

As Agafon plodded up the beach to the camp trail, I ran to the rocky outcrops that stretched out a hundred yards into the bay. With my burlap bag slung over a shoulder, I worked my way out on the rocks on the opposite side so no one could see me and found a good place where the water looked deep. I unrolled one of the lines, tossed out the baited and weighted hook, and sat down. A minute later I felt a tug on the line. I couldn't believe it. I already had a fish. Suddenly, the line began to move. I yanked hard and pulled in the line, hand over hand, until the fish was at the surface, flapping and splashing, trying to get off the hook. It was a flounder. I pulled it up onto the rocks and killed it. The little bait fish was still on the hook, though somewhat mangled. I tossed out the line out again and soon caught another flounder, this one even larger than the first. By the time the sun started to go down, I had caught three flounder and a cod. I carried them back to camp on a stick poked through the gills and mouth, the way Father had taught me at fish camp, and hid them behind a tree along with my fishing bag, which I covered with moss and a few pieces of wood so no one would find it.

I found Agafon inside the cannery sitting by the wood stove.

"I caught four fish," I whispered into his ear, my voice full of excitement and pride.

"Good for you," he replied, slapping his knee with one hand. "Leave fish where people find them, but let no one see you and tell no one."

"But I want Father and Peter to see how I'm helping," I grumbled.

"No. You must not."

Agafon warned me that if I was discovered, the Keepers would restrict my movements, and then I wouldn't be able to help anymore, and our people would continue to suffer.

"You must swallow you pride, Kiska. It not about you. It about helping others. A true act of giving must be done without reward or recognition. You must gain nothing. A great chief must know this. *You* know what you do . . . that all that matters."

I thought about how Father always told me the same thing.

I did as Agafon said, and not even ten minutes later a man came in with the fish, telling how he had found them lying in the middle of the trail to the outhouse. It seemed like everyone in the cannery gathered around to see. People were asking who had caught the fish. Like a practiced actor, Agafon stood up and warned that the Keepers must not find out, otherwise they would take the fish for themselves. He said we should eat them before Mr. Anderson found out. The other elders nodded in agreement. That evening we all enjoyed fish chowder. There were many conversations about where the fish had come from.

I smiled every time I overheard one of the elders say Raven must be providing for us.

CHAPTER 9
The Winter of Our Sorrow

There wasn't much snow on the ground during December in 1942. But lack of snow doesn't mean lack of cold. The cannery had been built to operate only during the summer months, when enormous schools of salmon returned to the bays and inlets to spawn in such abundance that the mouths of rivers and streams were clogged. There had been no need to insulate the building. The cannery was so drafty that no amount of wood in the wood stove kept the spacious building above freezing. Day and night we could see our breath whenever we complained about the lack of heat.

"If we just had a wood stove on the other end of the cannery, maybe it would be warm enough," elders complained to Mr. Anderson, who always gave the same reply.

"I'm sorry, but I can't do nothin' about that," he'd say, shrugging his shoulders. "My hands are tied."

But, while we were freezing to death, Mr. Anderson and the other Keepers sat inside their nice warm cottage playing cards in their white undershirts smoking pipes or cigarettes and drinking piping hot coffee while listening to the radio.

Peter hated the Keepers for the way their lives were so comfortable while ours were so miserable. That night, while the Keepers slept in their nice warm beds, Peter climbed up a tree next to their cottage, crept across the shingled roof, and stuffed a wadded-up old coat into the chimney pipe. He quickly climbed back down the tree and returned to his bed on the cannery floor. A few minutes later, every one of the Keepers came tripping out the door, coughing and choking and rubbing their burning eyes.

Peter snickered when we all heard them.

I asked what was so funny, and he told me what he had done.

It *was* kind of funny.

But Peter's mischiefs did nothing to warm the drafty cannery. The never-ending cold affected the oldest among us the most. Umma's health worsened every day. Her coughs rattled in her thin chest. Sometimes she couldn't stop coughing. And she was always shivering. She didn't even get out of bed anymore. There were others in the same condition—too sick even to get up to go to the outhouse. Mother and several other women took care of the many sick—the comforting, the feeding, the endless cleaning. And when they pleaded with Mr. Anderson to send for a doctor, the answer was always the same as the one he gave about a wood stove.

"I'm sorry, but I can't do nothin' about that," he'd say,

zipping up his warm, Army-issue parka all the way to his chin. To his way of thinking, he was doing the best he could for his fellow Americans.

One day I sat with my Umma for half the day. Donia sat with her for the other half. Umma had four blankets heaped on her to keep her warm: mine, Mother and Father's, and Donia's. She looked so small in the blankets. For the most part, she slept between coughing fits, some so painful for her that I thought she'd die right then. When she was awake I tried to get her to drink hot broth to warm her insides and to help build strength. At one point she took my hand and pulled me close.

"You a good granddaughter," she half-whispered through the wheezing.

For a long time we talked about our lives before the war. We talked about how much we missed home. Umma talked about how much she missed Uppa, my grandfather. Then she got a serious look on her face and changed the subject.

"Take me home after I die. I don't want to be here. I want to lie beside my husband behind the church. Promise me."

"You're not going to die," I said in that reassuring tone we use even when we know it's a lie.

"Promise me," she said grabbing my wrist and then going into another coughing spasm.

When she was calm, I leaned over and kissed her forehead, burning hot.

"I promise." I smiled bravely, my eyes welling with

tears. I felt utterly helpless and, also, brimming with love.

I couldn't imagine life without my grandmother. She had always been part of it, every single day.

• • • •

I continued to fish every day.

On some days I caught so many fish that it took me two trips to haul all them all back to the cannery. But lately, I had returned more than once empty-handed, and complaints of hunger joined our conversations about the cold. Agafon said the fish had moved out to deeper water because of winter. I don't know if that's true. Maybe I had just caught all the fish near the rocky outcrop. One day I went looking for Agafon and found him carrying a small armful of sticks to feed to the hungry wood stove. He was bundled up wearing two coats with his green blanket draped over his head and shoulders like a shawl and with a pair of black socks for gloves. I told him that I needed to learn some other method for catching food. Agafon thought about my request while I followed him into the cannery, picking up dropped sticks along the way.

"Today, I show you how to make crab trap," he said, after dropping the wood onto a small pile beside the stove. "Crab taste mighty good."

Ransacking the tool shed again, we borrowed a hatchet and snitched some of the white cotton cord, the same cord that I used as fishing line. Far enough away from camp so that no one would hear what we were doing, Agafon showed me how to build the trap. I cut four stout sticks about three feet long and laid them out in a square, tying the ends together with cord. Then, using other pieces of wood the same length, I laid them across the square frame, spaced about a thumb width apart, and secured them. When that was done, Agafon had me tie a length of rope, about four feet long, to each corner. Finally, I was instructed to tie the ends together into one knot and to the knot tie a long cord about fifty or sixty feet long.

"Now you need bait," he said, handing me a paper sack containing the tail fins and heads cut from several fish I had caught the day before.

He showed me how to fix the bait so that crabs had to stay on the trap to eat.

"Lower trap to bottom and wait for hour, then pull up . . . slowly. You catch crabs."

And he was right. I caught two crabs on my first try. Crabs aren't smart enough to know that they're being pulled up from the seafloor if you do it slowly. They just keep on greedily eating the bait, pinching at other crabs. They didn't live for long once they were out of the water.

I hid the crab trap beside my burlap fishing bag underneath a deadfall and covered it with moss and twigs and a large branch so no one would find it. I was on my way back to camp when I saw one of the Keepers coming toward me on the trail. He hadn't noticed me yet, so I casually tossed the crabs into a bush and kept on walking. When we were close on the narrow path the man stopped me. He was stoop-shouldered with a face like a hatchet, sharp and angular. His eyes looked like they were too close together, the space between his nose and eyes dark. All in all, he had a face like a rat.

"What are you doing here?" he grumbled in a nasally voice. "You're not supposed to be this far away from camp."

"I was just playing when I got lost. I sure am glad to see you," I lied with a disarming, helpless, lost-in-the-woods look of worry.

The man looked me up and down, sizing me up.

"Stay on the trail. It leads back to camp. And don't let me catch you out here again."

"Yes sir . . . and thank you!" I replied with false enthusiasm as the hatchet-faced rat-man continued down the trail, without looking back and without noticing the crabs on the side of the trail.

When I arrived in camp, I left the crabs where someone was sure to find them. I never left the things I caught in the same place twice for fear that someone might lie in wait to find me out. Maintaining my secret meant being sneaky. I was good at it.

• • • •

That night my Umma died in her sleep. She was frozen through and through when we found her in the morning, her eyes wide open, her hands—claw-like—clutched at her chest as if to grasp her escaping life. The Keepers carried her out like a plank of wood and buried her in a small ravine in the dark, suffocating forest behind the cannery. Little did we know at the time that the place was to become a monument to our despair and suffering.

My family had already suffered two losses to our imprisonment. Other families would suffer similar losses. Some would suffer worse.

Little by little, our hearts were being turned into cemeteries.

CHAPTER 10
To Catch a Sneak

While we listened to the wind beating against the thin cannery walls, the Keepers sat inside their cozy cottage listening to Glenn Miller and his band playing on the radio. We could hear the loud music even above the icy wind.

"I need your help," Peter whispered while I was helping Donia prepare the tables for breakfast.

"What do you want?" I asked, dressed in two coats to stay warm.

"Outside," said Peter, nodding toward the door.

I followed my brother outside.

"I need your help," said Peter, looking around to see if anyone was listening.

I didn't really want to help my brother. He'd been in trouble with the Keepers more times than I could keep track of. He had recently untied one of the supply boats that delivered the Keepers' weekly supply of beer, steaks, chocolate, and newspapers and magazines. It was half a mile adrift out to sea when they discovered what had happened. Like usual, Peter was suspected. Someone said they had seen him lurking around the dock beforehand.

Before that, Peter broke into the Keeper's stash of beer and poured every one of them onto the ground. He wanted to make sure that they were as miserable as we were. But two soldiers caught him red-handed as he was emptying the last bottle. They gave him a pretty good beating for that. I bet the Keepers wished Peter had been left back on our island and out of their hair.

But he was my brother.

"What do you need me to do?" I asked reluctantly, certain I would regret it later.

"Nothing really. I just need you to distract the Keepers for a few minutes."

"What are you going to do?"

"You'll see," he said, flashing one of his sly smiles.

"Don't worry, Sis. You won't get in trouble."

Next thing I knew I was setting fire to a little pile of kerosene-soaked rags in a bucket, which was strategically placed behind the Keeper's cottage.

"Fire! Fire!" I shouted while knocking on the cottage door.

While the Keepers were outside putting out the fire, Peter stole into the cottage and pulled out one of the vacuum tubes from inside the radio. He wore gloves so as not to burn his hands. Without the sealed glass tube, the radio wouldn't work. The lights would come on, but no broadcast could be received.

Now they would have only the hollow wind to listen to.

But Peter made a mistake. He kept the vacuum tube as a souvenir, hiding it in my bedding after we all got up for the day. Mr. Anderson ordered all of us to stand outside in the freezing cold, while his men searched the cannery. One of them found the tube. I saw him talking to Mr. Anderson, and then they both looked at me. Mr. Anderson scowled.

"Kiska Baranoff!" he shouted. "Come here!"

He showed me the tube and accused me of stealing it and of creating the fire. He grabbed me by the wrist and pulled me roughly toward the tool shed.

"I'll teach you to steal from me," he said.

"Please. I didn't do it," I pleaded, struggling to free myself.

But Peter ran after us and grabbed Mr. Anderson by the shoulder and spun him around. Two guards ran up to subdue Peter.

"She didn't do it!" he shouted. "I did it."

Mr. Anderson released his grip on my wrist. I fell to the ground.

"Is that so?" he said.

"My sister had nothing to do with it. I started the fire. I stole the stupid tube."

With a nod from Mr. Anderson, the two guards grabbed Peter and dragged him kicking to the tool shed.

"Two days," said Mr. Anderson, as he closed and locked the door with a chain.

But when one of the guards came to deliver Peter's breakfast the next morning, the shed was empty. He informed Mr. Anderson, who sent out a search party.

They caught Peter and threw him back into the shed. He was gone when they checked on him at suppertime. Another search was conducted, and Peter was again found and returned to his prison. This time, though, a guard was posted outside the shed. Sometime during the windy night, Peter escaped again.

I was present when they brought my brother back to camp. He was surrounded by weary Keepers. As they escorted Peter back to the shed, he turned and smiled at me.

This was all a game to Peter.

From where I stood, I watched as the guards shoved my brother into the shed, slammed and locked the door, double checking the chain and lock. They weren't thirty steps from the shed when I heard a twig snap. One of the guards turned just in time to see Peter creeping into the forest. I saw the guard turn, shake his head in disbelief . . . and admiration.

You had to admire my brother's tenacity.

I asked Peter later how he kept escaping.

"It was a snap," he boasted. "The floor was earthen. I used a shovel to dig a hole under the wall, just enough to wriggle though, you know. Then I reached in and slid a wooden crate over the hole. There was an empty fuel drum against the outside wall. I used it to hide the hole on the outside. I'm surprised they never found out. Not too bright, I guess."

• • • •

Peter wasn't the only one who wanted my help. Sasha

wanted to catch whoever was secretly bringing the fish, and he came to me of all people to help him do it.

"But *why* do you want to catch the person?" I asked.

"Don't *you* wanna know?" he replied.

"Not really. I'm just happy not to be hungry all the time."

"Well, I wanna find out who it is."

"What happens if you do?" I asked, wondering about Sasha's plans. "I mean, if Mr. Anderson finds out he'll put an end to it and we'll all go hungry again."

"I won't tell anyone else. I'm just bored out of my skull. There's nothing to do around here other than gathering firewood. Come on. It's a mystery. It'll be fun."

I reluctantly agreed to go along with Sasha's plan, thinking it'd be a distraction at any rate. I was pretty sure he wasn't going to catch me.

The first thing we did was to set trip lines made of empty cans with a few pebbles inside. We punched holes in the cans using a hammer and a nail and tied them low across the well-used paths before dark so that the loud rattling when someone tripped the lines would alert us to anyone coming or going. But that didn't work out very well; seems like an awful lot of folks peed in the woods at night instead of walking down the long, dark trail in the cold to use the outhouse at the end of the dock.

My parents put a stop to our trip alarms after a number of complaints.

The next day, after doing our morning chores, Sasha

and I hid along some of the main trails, concealing our-
selves behind spruce boughs we broke from low hanging branches. Of course, we got pretty cold from just
sitting there doing nothing, waiting. I swear my bottom
was frozen. I'd have gone back inside to warm up by the
woodstove if the idea of sitting there with Sasha wasn't
so hilarious. Needless to say, we didn't see anything or
anyone suspicious all day. We did see some squirrels
busily searching for nuts and chattering at us in our
hiding place. We weren't fooling them.

That night, ever determined to catch whoever it was,
Sasha had the bright idea to climb one of the trees at
the edge of the clearing around the cannery and wait
for the secret provider to show his face.

"We're gonna catch him tonight," said Sasha, rubbing his freezing ears.

"What makes you think it's a *he*?" I asked. "Maybe
it's a *she*."

"Don't be ridiculous. Girls can't fish."

"How hard can it be to catch fish?" I said sarcasti-
cally. "I mean, you throw a hook in the water and wait.
Real hard. Better call a he-man."

Sasha looked at me through furrowed brows, as if I
had just said that the sky was down instead of up, as if
I made no sense to him whatsoever.

"Maybe it's my sister, Donia, or that Galena?" I continued. "She's like twenty years old and built like a tree
trunk. She's pretty strong. I once saw her . . ."

"No way it's a girl," interrupted Sasha, shaking his
head in disbelief. "My bet is on Peter."

"Peter? Why is it so hard for you to believe a girl could do it? I asked, beginning to get angry at Sasha's attitude. "I carry as much firewood as you do. I haul the same heavy buckets of water. I can even run as fast as you," I said, remembering the time we raced down the trail to the dock to see who was faster.

I could see that Sasha remembered we tied.

"Yeah . . . but . . . but," he stuttered, thinking of the right words before I clobbered him, "men are just . . . well . . . *better* . . . at some things."

"Have you ever heard the story of Millie and Maura Secondchief?"

Sasha shook his head, indicating that he hadn't.

"Back around 1920, Natives all over Alaska were dying from a plague brought by the white people. So many people died that they call it The Great Death. Everyone in Millie and Maura's village died . . . *everyone*," I said, overstressing the last word. "I think Millie was my age and her sister, Maura, was only ten. They were the only ones left alive. For all they knew, they were the last two people on earth. But they were determined to survive."

As I related the story, I couldn't help but think of Agafon's childhood on the Island of Dogs.

"The way I heard it, they struck out into the wilderness in the middle of winter at, like, forty degrees below zero. They didn't even know where to go for sure, because they had never been away from their village. They decided to follow a river, hoping it would lead to other villages. They followed that frozen river for months, living off the land and avoiding wolves, just two small girls against the wilderness. It was amazing that they survived at all. Finally, after an amazing journey, they came upon a town full of white people."

"That sounds like a legend," replied Sasha.

"It's not a legend! It really happened!" I replied defensively. "It happened about twenty years ago. They're still alive. My mother met one of them at boarding school. I bet a boy their same age wouldn't have survived that journey."

Sasha was quiet after that, thinking about the story, imagining the hardships, envisioning wolves pursuing two girls through the whiteness of winter.

"I bet you never heard the story of Ada Blackjack, either?"

Again, Sasha shook his head.

"Ada was an Eskimo from Nome. She was the only woman on an expedition to explore the Arctic. It happened around the same time as The Great Death. Ada was only twenty years old, I think . . . maybe a little older. Anyhow, two years after they left, only Ada returned alive. She was the sole survivor. A girl, not a man."

"Is that a true story?"

"You can read about it. Newspapers around the world called her the female Robinson Crusoe," I boasted as if I were talking about my own mother or grandmother.

I could see from his face that Sasha was thinking about the things I had said, so I continued my effort to convince him that girls can do anything boys can do.

"Did you know that ever since the war began, women are working in factories, doing the same jobs men used to do? I heard about it on the radio. They're not making pink dresses or doilies. They're making bullets, machine guns, tanks, ships, airplanes, trucks and bull-dozers, bombs and bombers. They're welding and rivet-ing just like men."

"Maybe someday they'll tell stories about you," said Sasha.

I smiled at the thought.

For the next half hour, we sat in the tree debating male and female roles in society loud enough that any-one would have heard us. In the end, we got too cold and climbed down around midnight. Although I got Sasha thinking about things, about equality, I don't think he changed his mind that the crafty individual could possibly be a girl. He insisted it was my brother.

All the better for me, I guess. At least he wouldn't suspect me.

The next day, Sasha and I resumed our intrigues, sneaking around the cannery like spies, making our-selves as invisible as we could, taking mental notes of every coming and going, and watching for anything out of the ordinary. For the first time, I noticed something I hadn't before, something that involved my own sister.

Some of the other young women were secretly meet-ing with some of the Keepers behind the tool shed. Sasha and I found a spot to hide where we could see pretty well. We'd see them arrive separately—one of the young women from our group and one of the men who worked for Mr. Anderson. They'd stand very close at first, whispering to one another. The man would pull out a small bottle of liquor from inside his coat and show it to the young woman. Then, when they thought no one was looking, the man would go into the shed and close the door. A minute later, the young woman would casually go inside and close the door behind her. After a while, one of the two would peek out the door, making sure the coast was clear, and then depart. The other would do the same a few minutes after that. We watched this happen several times during the day. I was shocked when I saw Donia, my own sister, go into the shed with one of the leering men. The women always came out of the shed with their hair mussed and their blouses misbuttoned; the grinning men with their shirts untucked. By the end of the day there was a small pile of discarded alcohol bottles lying on the ground outside the shed.

Booze wasn't the only commodity traded for love, for lack of a proper word. Sometimes, we noticed the young women hiding and eating something, which turned out to be chocolate. We knew this because we'd find the wrappers crumpled on the ground. We also noticed that some of the women were wearing nylon stockings, which were wildly popular in the states. I had seen advertisements in magazines and in the Sears Roebuck catalog back in our village.

We spied on everyone all day and half the night.

I was exhausted the next day, having not slept well in days from all our antics. To make matters worse, I hadn't gone out to catch anything because Sasha was watching so closely. People started to complain about the absence of the mysterious fish. They were hungry again. It always surprised me that Sasha never put two and two together. I mean, no new food was delivered during those days that we were together. It reminded me of how Lois Lane never figured out how Clark Kent was always absent whenever Superman was around saving somebody or other.

I guess some people just can't see what they don't want to see.

CHAPTER 11
The Baidarka

"I want to build a kayak."

With a raised eyebrow, Agafon studied my face. I think he was waiting for a punch line.

"I need to go out to deeper water to catch fish. Will you help me?"

I could tell from his expression that Agafon was thinking.

"Alright," he said standing up slowly, "We make baidarka. We go see what we have around here to build one."

I knew that our baidarkas back home were made from tanned seal or sea lion skin, but I had no idea what we would use to make one here. In the back of the shed—where the white men and our young women met for their secret love play—Agafon found a large, folded oilcloth canvas that the Keepers had used as makeshift quarters before their cozy cottage was built. We took the canvas, as well as a few tools we needed, including sheers and a spool of white cord.

We decided to build the kayak in the woods near a little cove that was far from the cannery. Agafon and I worked on the kayak for days, cutting green saplings and bending them into the skeletal hull about eight feet long and just wide enough for me to sit inside. It was a small kayak, as kayaks go. We used cord to bind the frame. Over that, we stretched a piece of the canvas, cutting it to fit and stitching it together on top. I painted the outside of the canvas with a thin coat of black roofing tar from a partial five-gallon bucket we found in the shed. Agafon made a simple paddle from a seven-foot length of wood onto which he nailed an oval-shaped plywood palm on each end.

As we carried the kayak down to the beach—one of us at either end holding onto a looped cord at the bow and stern—I asked Agafon a question that had been bothering me.

"My father always tells me that girls aren't allowed to touch kayaks. He says it's our custom. He says it's taboo, whatever that means. How come you're letting me touch this one?"

Agafon laughed so loud he snorted.

"In old days, men thought kayak a living thing . . . thought them magic. Magic go away if woman touch it."

"But you don't think it's true nowadays?"

"Guess we see soon," he replied, nodding toward the sea. "Besides, girl make this kayak for girl."

He smiled and winked at me.

We gingerly sat the kayak at the water's lapping

edge. It looked fragile on land, but Agafon insisted it would float.

"Maybe not float for long time," he warned. "Take on water after a while. Stay close to shore, and take this with you," he said, handing me an empty coffee can he brought from camp.

"What's this for?" I asked skeptically.

"To bail water. Don't worry. You do fine."

I have to admit, I was a little unsure about the craft's seaworthiness, especially after Agafon's comment. But the first time I went out in it—staying close to shore while Agafon looked on, counseling me from the beach—my fears were eased. The little craft floated easily and it had a shallow draft. It floated on just a few inches of water. It responded effortlessly to my paddle. I had watched Father and Uncle enough to know the basics of paddling, including the back-paddle. I knew that no stroke was ever wasted. In no time at all, I waved goodbye to Agafon and struck out toward the middle of the little cove, dropped my fishing line into deeper water. Only a few minutes later I pulled up a small halibut. After that, I caught the ugliest fish I had ever seen. I kept it only to show Agafon. I also caught a small shark, about three feet long. I was afraid of the fearsome teeth, so I cut the line instead of trying to remove it. I hadn't expected to pull up a shark.

You never know what you'll catch in the sea.

By the time I returned to the beach where Agafon was waiting for me, I had caught four small halibut and a red snapper.

I showed Agafon the hideous fish.

"They call that Irish Lord. It not for eating," he said. "Be good bait, though."

As always, we gutted the fish there on the beach, cutting off the tails and other choice pieces to save for bait. We left the heads on because the elders loved fish head soup.

The kayak had taken on a little water, but not enough to bail. Agafon said it would take on more water as the tar dried. He instructed me to give the canvas a light coat once a month, more if it needed it, and to avoid poking a hole in the bottom whenever I moved it. He also told me to store it upside down, to keep it from filling from rainwater. I already knew that because we always stored our kayaks upside down on special racks made from driftwood. As I always did with my fishing bag, I concealed the kayak beneath a heap of spruce boughs so no one would find it.

Before walking back to the cannery for supper with our bounty of fish, Agafon knelt and gripped my shoulders.

"Promise me not to go out too far," he said earnestly. "This important. Stay close to beach. It dangerous to go out too far. I never forgive myself something happen to you. Promise me."

I could see that he was genuinely concerned.

"I promise."

Just then it began to drizzle, the light rain thickening with fog and wind.

Halfway back to camp, after walking up a somewhat

steep path, Agafon stumbled and fell. I helped him back to his feet.

"Are you alright?" I asked, steadying him.

"I need to sit down for a minute."

I led Agafon to a log and sat down beside him.

"What happened?" I asked.

"I got dizzy. Everything turn black."

"Do you want me to go get help?" I asked, knowing that no doctor ever came to help us.

"No, no. I be alright. Just sit for minute. Let old man catch his breath."

"It is kind of steep," I replied, looking up the trail. "Maybe we just need to go slower, that's all."

Agafon nodded.

"Maybe little slower be good. Just light-headed, I think."

After a few minutes, I helped Agafon up and, with the fish I had caught, we resumed our trek, stopping to rest along the way.

• • • •

The next day I went out again in my little kayak. The cove was flat, mirror-like, reflecting the beach and surrounding hills and the puffy clouds overhead. I paddled out to where I had caught fish the day before. And like before, I dropped a line over the side and fed out more line as the weight carried the fish-tail-baited hook to the seafloor. Once I could tell it was on the bottom, I pulled in a couple feet of cord so that dangling bait would be just off the bottom, attracting flat fish, like halibut or flounder, as well as cod or snappers, or anything else that might see or smell the hovering morsel.

It was such a beautiful, lazy day that I allowed myself to daydream, something I rarely did in those days. I started thinking about home, about gathering eggs in the green cliffs, about running along the beach with my dog who would run ahead of me flushing seagulls into the sky. I thought about listening to the radio with my family in the evening, me cradling Mary in my arms. I thought about how excited I was whenever Father and Uncle and the other men returned from seal hunting. I missed home. I missed our church. I missed my dog.

Suddenly, my serene daydream turned into anger.

Why did this happen to me? Why are we . . . why am I here? I hate this place. I hate the stupid cannery. I hate the way we're treated, the way Father isn't the strong man he used to be. I hate what's become of my sister. I hate all the senseless deaths. And I hate that we have to follow the Keeper's rules. Who are they to tell us what to do? They're not better than we are. They're nothing but a bunch of thugs and bullies. I didn't ask for all this! I don't want it! I hate the stupid war! I just want to go home!

I was angry at the whole world for taking my life away from me, possibly forever. My rage was so great that I bit my lower lip. I wiped my chin with a hand, looking at my bloody palm, trembling with anger.

Suddenly, I felt a powerful yank on the line, so forceful that it almost tipped me over. Then the line began to move. I tried to pull in whatever it was I had caught, but no matter how hard I strained, I was unable to pull in even a single foot of the cotton cord. Then, whatever it was began to pull me in my kayak out of the cove, toward open water. Looking at the shoreline and at trees, I was amazed at how fast I was moving, almost as fast as I could run. Whatever it was pulled my kayak out of the cove and around the bend.

I began to wonder what the heck I had hooked.

Was it a whale? A sea monster?

I remember wondering if I had snagged one of the small, two-man Japanese submarines we had heard about in the news.

Whatever it was, it was pulling me out to sea. In a matter of minutes, I must have been a thousand yards from land. Out on the sea, the wind was stronger than it had been in the protected cove, and the frightening waves heaved and rolled beneath me. I realized I could be pulled so far away that I'd never be able to make it back. The strong tides could make it even more difficult, even impossible. I'd be lost . . . or worse. For the first time, I realized that I was no more than a speck of dust on the vast and briny deep.

Remembering my promise to Agafon, I let go of the line. I watched as the remaining length of white cord was instantly swallowed by the sea.

Using my paddle, I turned the craft and struck out homeward. I was relieved as the distance between myself and land closed. As I rounded the bend back into the cove, I saw otters floating amid kelp. One was on its back eating something.

Then I saw the seals.

They swam close to investigate me, just their sleek heads and black eyes visible. I tossed out a fish tail. One of them came closer, diving where the bait had splashed, and then surfacing a moment later with the silvery tail in its mouth. The sleek, beautiful creature was so close I could see its whiskers and sharp, white teeth. I remember wondering if this was how it was for Father and Uncle when they went out to hunt seals.

After returning to the cannery, empty-handed, I found Agafon and told him what happened. I didn't tell him how far out to sea I had been pulled. I didn't want to worry him.

"What do you think it was?" I asked. "What could be that big?"

"Maybe salmon shark. They grow big, almost thousand pounds. Maybe giant halibut. They get big as a sheet of plywood. I seen one almost five hundred pounds."

We sat for a few minutes thinking about what else it might have been. I didn't mention sea monsters or Japanese submarines.

"Maybe it was a submerged log? Nah. There was no current in the cove that could have carried a log like that," I said, answering my own question.

We were quiet for another few minutes again.

"I saw seals," I said, changing the subject.

Agafon's eyes lit up.

"I miss seal meat," he replied, using the Aleut word.

"Teach me how to hunt them," I said.

Agafon smiled and nodded.

"I teach you."

CHAPTER 12
We the People

Even though my father and uncle and the other men in my village use rifles to hunt seals nowadays, I had to use something else. I didn't think the Keepers would loan me a gun. Agafon told me to make a spear and to practice . . . a lot. He said not to worry about the point yet.

"First you need learn throw straight," he had instructed me.

I'll be honest—even after days of practicing I couldn't throw the spear straight for anything. I was getting discouraged. But then I got the idea to ask Father and Uncle.

"Why do you need to know?" Uncle asked.

"There's nothing to do around here," I lied. "I thought I'd pretend to be a seal hunter like in the old days."

At first Father and Uncle took turns, showing me where to hold the spear, how to balance it. They talked about the length and thickness.

"You need a longer spear, thinner," said Father.

"Hold it further back . . . here," instructed Uncle. "And hold your other arm out like this, for balance."

They took turns throwing it at a target on the ground. They told me other things about seal hunting like how a wounded seal will sometimes swim down to the bottom of the ocean to die, robbing the hunter of his prize.

"You have to paddle fast after you get one, before it go down," Father warned.

But then a funny thing happened—the other men standing around started getting involved.

"It should have more flex," one man said.

"It should be more stiff," said another.

"Don't grip it so tight," instructed an old man.

Next thing I knew, the young men were searching the woods for suitable spears to throw. The older men had their children or grandchildren search for them.

"Longer than that," they would say.

"No, that one too dry."

Soon, everyone was standing around watching as the men threw their spears at the same target, trying to see who came closest. The audience applauded and cheered. There was good-natured jeering.

"My grandmother throws better than you," someone shouted when a spear sailed far left of the target.

For the first time in a long time there was laughter at the cannery. Even the younger boys were having their own contest.

I took in all the instruction, watching and listening.

Even now, I remember the joy of that moment. For however briefly, we had reconnected to who we are inside: Aleuts. Sometimes a drop of happiness can stave off a sea of despair.

• • • •

A few days later, one of the Keepers found a heap of fish bones in the woods behind the cannery. Our cooks had made the mistake of throwing all the leftover bones in one place. In retrospect, it's easy to see that they should have buried them. The man showed his discovery to Mr. Anderson, who quickly figured that a pile of fish bones meant that someone was breaking the rules by leaving camp to catch the fish. If someone could sneak away so easily, they could escape, and that would look bad on his record. With his hat askew and his ubiquitous corn cob pipe in his mouth, Mr. Anderson called his staff and ordered them to search the entire camp, leaving no bed unturned. They made us line up outside in the cold while the men rummaged through everything, even shaking out all the bedding. When they found nothing suspicious in the cannery, they started checking our persons.

I don't think they knew exactly what they were looking for. They must have figured they'd know what it was when they found it.

I was nervous.

Earlier that morning, Agafon and I had fashioned three new fish hooks from nails, tying the little loops to the ends. I often lost hooks when they snagged on rocks or logs. I had them inside my right coat pocket, wrapped in a handkerchief to keep them from poking through. I also had a file I kept for sharpening the points when they dulled. I had lost fish because of dull hooks. I also had my jackknife in the same pocket. If they found them on me, they would put a stop to my excursions.

One of the men grabbed me.

"You got anything on you that you shouldn't?" he barked

His breath smelled sour from too much coffee.

I winced and shook my head.

"What's this?" he said, grabbing my sea lion amulet and pulling it close to inspect it.

"It's just a necklace."

"It looks nice," he said. "Genuine Native art. I think I'll take it."

I was scared and angry at the same time. The necklace was too important to me . . . to my people. I wouldn't be able to hunt or catch fish without its magic powers. I wasn't going to let him steal it from me. I slapped his hand away hard and stepped back, ready for anything.

"You can't have it!" I screamed. "It's mine!"

The man stepped toward me, his scowling face turning red. He grabbed me roughly and dragged me back into the lineup.

"Let's see what else you got," the man said as he felt the outside pockets of my pants, front and back. Feeling nothing, he reached into my left coat pocket. My body stiffened and I held my breath when he was about to plunge his hand into my right pocket, the one with the hooks and knife. Just then, one of the other Keepers interrupted him.

"Leave her. She's just a girl."

The man looked me over and then moved on to frisk the next person in line.

I breathed a sigh of relief.

Agafon was right when he said they wouldn't suspect a girl.

A scuffle began a few minutes later when one of the soldiers got a little too personal while feeling one of the young women who was married. She and her husband came from one of the Pribilof Islands. I think it was St. Paul. Their last name was Zacharof. Her husband shoved the soldier and told him to leave his wife alone. Two other soldiers ran over, and together, all three of them beat the Aleut man almost to death. While he was lying on the ground protecting his head with his arms, they continued to kick him, shouting things like, "We're gonna teach you animals a lesson."

The Keepers were always saying that we weren't really people, even though we didn't look that much different from most of them. Many of us, me included, were part White. I remember one time when a soldier came to deliver a plate full of bones.

"Here's some bones for you dogs," he said as he callously spilled them on the cannery floor for us to pick up to make soup broth.

I was furious.

As the man walked the trail back toward the Keeper's warm cottage, I hurled a rock at him, just missing his head. When he turned around I was gone, hiding behind a tree.

Later that day, while walking along the beach, Sasha and I saw Agafon sitting on a rock close to the beach's high tide mark. He looked so alone out there all by himself. I told Sasha I wanted to go talk to him.

"You know him?" he replied.

"Oh, I talk to him sometimes."

"You shouldn't talk to that old man. I've heard weird things about him."

"Like what?"

"People say he's crazy," said Sasha. "I heard someone say that he killed his whole village a long time ago. Killed them all, even the dogs. Then he ate them."

I laughed, especially after hearing the last part.

"That's just gossip. Don't believe everything you hear," I said. "Anyway, I'm going to talk to him. You can go back to camp if you're afraid."

"I'm not afraid," Sasha boasted.

But I noticed he stayed several steps behind me as we walked up to Agafon.

"What are you doing?" I asked.

"Just watching tide come in. I like this spot."

"You look so lonely."

"Loneliness is to be poor of spirit," said Agafon, a sea breeze blowing his long white hair across his face. "I not lonely. Simply embracing solitude. Very different."

I thought about what he said, how I felt lonely sometimes.

"Who is your friend?" asked Agafon, trying to look at Sasha standing behind me.

"Say hello, Sasha. Come on, he doesn't bite."

Sasha stepped out reluctantly, his head hanging down as if he was studying pebbles on the beach.

"Hey," is all he said.

"Hmph. Big talker," said Agafon.

"Did you see what happened to Mr. Zacharof?" I asked.

Agafon nodded that he had.

"The Keepers say we're animals . . . that we're not human."

"You know that not true, Kiska," he said. "What our name in Aleut?"

"*Unangan*," I said, proud that I knew the word.

"And what it mean?"

I thought for a minute.

"I don't remember," I finally replied feeling embarrassed.

Agafon smiled softly at me the way he always did.

"It mean *We the People*. We *are* people. They know that. But it easier for them to say we not."

"They say we're animals, but then they sneak around with our women," I said angrily, thinking about Donia going into the shed with the soldier. "I feel like I wanna . . . I wanna . . . *do* something to them. I want to make them pay for the way they treat us."

"Better to show kindness."

"But why? They haven't been kind to us."

"It easy to be kind to friends and family. True test

showing kindness to folks that don't like you or can't do nothing for you."

Something in Agafon's voice or in his words struck Sasha. He looked up and stared at the old man.

"But *why* is kindness so important?" I asked. "People say it's important to be tough. My uncle is always saying *every man for himself*."

"My dad always says to look out for number one," Sasha interjected.

"That how some people see life. But there a better way to live."

Agafon picked up a pine cone, held it up for us to see.

"While it possible to count all seeds in this pine cone," he said," it *impossible* to count all the pine trees in one seed."

Seeing that we didn't understand, Agafon struck the cone against his palm.

"Kindness is like a seed you plant," he said with an open hand, showing us the seeds that had fallen out. "You never know how the fruit of kindness affect future. Better to repay unkindness with kindness."

To reinforce the lesson, Agafon picked up a pebble and tossed it into the encroaching tide. We watched as rings of ripples raced outward from the splash.

"Kindness like them waves. It start one place, with one person, but go out from there."

None of us spoke for a long time.

"Why is God doing this to us?" I asked in a small and earnest voice. "Does he hate us?"

Agafon looked at me in a way he never had before. I don't know how to describe it. He looked *through* me.

"Sometimes God want to make us stronger. That why he put trouble in our path. But remember this, you two: the troubles in our lives not obstacles; they just life."

I can't speak for Sasha, but it took me a long time to understand what Agafon meant.

I still wrestle with it.

CHAPTER 13
Death Unleashed

Spring shuffled in as if exhausted from the long winter. Slowly, the days grew longer as the sun slid higher into the sky above the towering trees that tried to seize all the light for themselves. Birds were busy singing and making nests. Leaves began to unfurl, insects buzzed in the warming air, and green stalks of wild flowers willed themselves from darkness into light. Everywhere, life was renewing.

But spring's promise of better days ahead was a lie.

One morning, a little boy named Nikolai awoke with red spots on his forehead. By noon his face was covered. He complained how the spots itched. By late afternoon, his fever rose so high that he had a seizure. At first the elders thought he had eaten something poisonous, strange berries perhaps. Others said he might be allergic to something in the air. We had never lived away from our islands in the springtime.

"Could be anything," said one elderly woman.

Others nodded their heads in agreement.

"Could be pollen from the trees," suggested one man.

"Yes," replied another hopefully. "Could be pollen."

As they spoke about possibilities, the elders felt better about the boy's prospects.

But Agafon shook his head sadly. He had an idea of what it was. He had met it before . . . when he was a boy.

"Look in his mouth," he instructed me.

"What for?" I asked.

"See if there white spots with blue and white in middle."

I asked the concerned mother if I could look inside her son's mouth. She told the miserable boy to let me see. The roof of his mouth had the spots just as Agafon had described. I reported what I had seen.

Agafon shook his head sadly.

"The red spots kill everyone in my village," he whispered. "They kill everyone here now."

I shuddered remembering the story Agafon had told me.

"Are you sure?" I asked.

"We see soon enough."

Agafon was right. The next day the red spots covered the little boy's head and chest. His eyes were red and he began to have what seemed like a really bad cold. A committee of elders told Mr. Anderson about the boy, urging him to get a doctor. But Mr. Anderson refused to send for a doctor.

"The doctor is very busy in Juneau. There's a bad cold going around town," he said. "He can't drop everything and come here to examine a bunch of people with a rash."

The next day, several other children in camp had the spots, which seemed to start at the hairline and work their way down the face from there. They also had the spots inside their mouths. We showed Mr. Anderson, who still didn't send for a doctor. By the fourth day, dozens of us had the red spots, young and old alike. By now, the little boy who had it first was covered from head to toe and front to back. He coughed all the time and wheezed when he breathed, the way little Mary coughed before she died on the ship.

I think he was drowning inside.

Mr. Anderson finally requested a doctor, but no doctor ever came.

Within two weeks, one hundred and eighteen of us had caught the red spots. I know it was that number exactly because Uncle had asked me to go around camp to count the sick so that he could tell Mr. Anderson. Mother and Father caught it, but Donia and I didn't. Everywhere the sick lay on the floor coughing and scratching and crying, their weepy and crusted red eyes fearful to look at. Day and night inside the cannery was the mumbling of prayers. Those of us without the spots took care of the sick, cooling their burning bodies with damp clothes, spoon-feeding them to keep their strength up, and carting away the sloshing buckets of waste to dump at the outhouse.

I sometimes still have nightmares about those horrible buckets.

I grew convinced that we were all going to die, and I'm sure others felt the same way. The dread was sculpted into their faces. But we noticed that none of the white people caught the spots. None of them got sick.

Not a single one.

. . . .

Agafon had been right about the spots, about the death they would bring. Nikolai was the first to die. He was only three. His father buried him in the cemetery beside my Umma. But they weren't alone for long. Day after day the cemetery filled with graves of the very young and the very old. I remember what one of the Keepers said to us one day as we were standing over the freshly filled graves for our families.

"You brought it down on yourselves," he admonished us. "God's punishing you for your godless ways."

I remember how angry that made me. We prayed to the same God as he did . . . *as they all did.* In every way that mattered, our beautiful church back home was the same as theirs wherever they came from. What angered me even more was his blindness to the misery they inflicted on us, to our suffering and dying. Where was the love and kindness and compassion they were taught about each Sunday?

Do unto others as you would have them do unto you.

Blessed are the poor.

Love thy neighbor.

And worst of all, he must have known—as we understood with increasing anger—that the terrible, killing spots came from him and his people, from our close proximity to each other for so long. It was *they* who gave them to us, they who were killing us without the slightest gesture of pity.

Even though I and others spent our days and half our nights caring for the sick—especially, on my part, for my own family—I still had to find time to supplement our "secret" food, so that we could keep up what little strength we had. What had begun as an exciting adventure was becoming more of a necessity, a matter of survival. One day when I went down to the little cove where I hid my kayak I saw something amazing. The sea was swarming with herring, millions of them. The little stream that ran into the cove was clogged with the skinny fish.

Here was food enough to feed the world, I thought.

I fashioned my gunny sack into a makeshift net, fixing it to the end of a long, forked tree limb. The mouth of the net was more triangular than circular, but it worked just as well. I positioned myself on the right side of a boulder in the creek, downriver where a deep eddy formed. With a single dip into the teeming water, the sack filled with bright, wriggling fish. It was so heavy that I couldn't even carry it. I poured half the fish into the belly of my kayak and carried the rest back to camp, the sack slung over my shoulder making me feel like pictures I had seen of Santa Claus, a saint who also bore gifts. Even with the haul divided in half, the load bore me down, but it was a happy burden. I was so exhausted from the first trip and from days of endlessly attending to the sick that when I returned for the rest of the fish, I fell asleep beside the kayak. I must have slept for hours, for when I awoke the sun stood tip-py-toe on the lip of the sea.

I hurried back with my second gunnysack haul of herring.

• • • •

The days back then are now a blur. There was so much misery, so much sadness, toil, and exhaustion. Even now, it's hard to separate the memories of one day from the next. But I remember that we buried our relatives daily, nine in one terrible day alone. I found a little time each day to return to the cove to net more herring. Those shimmering little fish were a godsend, arriving so plentifully when they did and so easy to catch. Within a few days they had disappeared, as I knew they must, as quickly and completely as they had appeared. The only evidence that they had ever been there was their eggs, which clung to everything beneath the waves.

By the time the season of spots had passed, almost a hundred of us had died.

CHAPTER 14
Birthday Girl

One day, I noticed one of the Keepers reading a newspaper at a table. I saw it was dated June 4, 1943. I wasn't sure of the date that day, so I asked him how old the paper was. He said it was a day old. That meant that my fifteenth birthday was only a few days away. It also meant that it had been almost a year since we were evacuated from our village. I couldn't believe a whole year had gone by.

Around lunchtime, Mr. Anderson called an assembly in the cannery. Everyone was required to attend. As we all found places to sit or stand, the Keepers stood along the walls armed with rifles. When everyone was ready, Mr. Anderson cleared his throat and spoke to us from atop a chair so that he could be seen and heard throughout the large room.

"Your government needs your help. We all have to make sacrifices to defeat the Nazis and the Japs."

Everyone listened attentively. We all wanted the war to end so we could go home.

"We wanna send most of you men back to St. Paul and St. George to harvest fur seals for the war effort. We need their fur for the liners of flight jackets and flight helmets. It's cold up there in those bombers and fighters. Our fly boys need to stay warm to continue the good fight and send our enemies to hell."

We all nodded.

The men smiled at the thought of going home to harvest fur seals, a practice that began when the Aleuts were forced to labor on the Pribilof Islands in the Bering Sea after the Russian fur traders had discovered the fabled and uninhabited seal breeding grounds in 1786. For almost a hundred years, the Aleuts were virtually enslaved on the islands to harvest seals for the Russian-American Company.

"Now, it'll just be for a month or two, during the breeding season, but you'll be home and you'll be well fed. Uncle Sam would sure appreciate your cooperation on this one."

One of the men raised his hand.

"Yes?" said Mr. Anderson, pointing at the man.

The man stood up to ask his question, his gray hat in hand.

"What if we don't go? I mean, I don't want to leave my wife and daughter here alone," he said, gazing at the armed soldiers leaning against the walls, coolly smoking cigarettes.

The cannery filled with whispering.

"Quiet! Quiet!" Mr. Anderson shouted.

"I'm authorized to tell you that if you don't go, then

the United States Government will not allow any of you to go home after the war."

The room turned deathly silent.

I have no idea whether Mr. Anderson was telling the truth or not, but he was the voice of the government in that place, among us who had no home and no rights. I couldn't find a way not to believe him.

"That's the deal," Mr. Anderson continued. "Volunteer like good Americans and you will all go home to your villages after the war. If you don't, you will *never* see your homes again. You will all be relocated to the States."

The silence was shattered by men shouting and shaking their fists, women crying and pleading with their husbands.

"Quiet!" Mr. Anderson shouted again.

But the raucous noise didn't settle. The armed soldiers moved into the center of the room, menacing us with their rifles. One soldier jabbed an Aleut man in the stomach with the butt of his rifle, sending him to his knees, where he tried to catch his breath.

The room finally quieted again.

"Will we be paid for our work?" asked a man from St. Paul.

"No," replied Mr. Anderson. "You will *contribute* your labor to the war effort."

Even though I was a couple days shy of fifteen, I understood that history has a way of repeating itself. First it was the Russians. . . .

KISKA

. . . .

The next morning, a ship arrived to take the select-
ed men back to the Pribilof Islands for the summer.
As the ship weighed anchor and pulled away from the
dock, mothers and wives and children waved at the men
standing on deck, hanging onto the railing, their coat
collars turned up against the wind. We all stood on the
dock watching until the ship was too far away to see.
The red spots cost us about a hundred people, mostly
the old and very young. Now, we were losing most of
the men. Those that remained were not from the Pribilofs, men like Father and Uncle and Sasha's father. The
rest of our sad little community was made up mostly of
children, the old and infirm, and women, Mother and
Donia included. Most of the teenage boys were left behind as well. Sasha was among them.

And of course, all of us teenage girls remained.

. . . .

For the next two days, I hunted seal. I was determined
to be a seal hunter like my father. But it was harder
than I imagined. Whenever I paddled my kayak close
enough to throw my spear, the seals would dive and
surface far away. I'd paddle over to where they were and
they'd dive again. It was like a game of cat and mouse.
When I tried to catch them bathing in the sun on a
rookery, they'd slide off the edge into the water just
as I'd throw the spear, which would harmlessly strike
the rock, breaking the point. The effortless quickness of

their moves always amazed me. I recalled what Father once told me: *Girls aren't allowed to touch a kayak. It brings bad luck.*

Maybe he was right.

Instead of seal meat, I returned to camp with seagull eggs I collected on a small, grassy island.

I told Agafon about my frustration.

"I'll never be a seal hunter. I'm just a failure," I said, feeling sorry for myself and looking down in shame.

At a place like Funter Bay, it wasn't hard to feel sorry for yourself.

Agafon gently placed his fingers beneath my chin and raised my head so he could look at my face.

"Failure only failure if you don't get up and try again," he said. "You daddy didn't get seal first time. Took him long time to get one."

I tried to imagine my father an incompetent hunter. That just seemed silly, almost funny.

"You smart girl. I bet you learn faster," he said and smiled.

I smiled back.

Agafon always knew what to say to make me feel better.

• • • •

That evening, my family sang "Happy Birthday" to me during dinner time. Everyone joined in and applauded at the end. There were no presents, of course, and no birthday cake with candles like at my last birthday back home. After dinner, I was walking back from the outhouse at the end of the dock when two Keepers stopped me on the trail. They stood close, too close, preventing me from passing. I recognized one of them as the rat-faced man I had met on the trail when I was bringing the crabs back to camp. The other man was new. I had never seen him before. He was short and thick with thin red hair.

Keepers came and went at Funter Bay. Only we Aleuts were permanent residents, we who had no home. The absence of so many of our men—fathers, husbands, uncles, brothers, and cousins—emboldened the Keepers' attention to our female population. Taking advantage of the situation, they began to harass us to no end.

I knew what they wanted.

"Well, well. Look who it is . . . The birthday girl," said the rat-faced man, his voice mean and small, like a rusty pocketknife.

"We heard you turned fifteen," said the other man, who ran his fingers through my hair. "You sure are a pretty little thing."

"Don't touch me!" I snapped, pulling my hair free.

I tried to walk around them, but they blocked my way.

"Where you going?" said Rat Face, grabbing my arm. "We just wanna talk to you."

"Let go of me!" I demanded, as I yanked my arm free.

I tried to push my way through them, but they grabbed me, one of them pinning my arm behind my back.

"That hurts," I cried out.

"Don't be like that," Rat Face whispered in my ear. "You're just gonna make it harder on yourself."

"Yeah. We just want to celebrate with you," said the other man as he pulled out a small bottle of liquor from inside his jacket. "Let's drink to your birthday."

Both men looked nervously up and down the trail to see if anyone was coming.

"I've had my eye on you ever since I got here," said the man with the bottle.

I tried to scream for help, but one of them held his hand over my mouth. I struggled to free myself, but the men were too strong. They laughed contemptuously.

Just then I heard a *thwack* and the man holding the bottle fell over. Rat Face looked at his friend in bewilderment, but before he could turn to see what had happened, I heard another *thwack* and Rat Face collapsed in a heap. Sasha stood over the two unconscious bodies, holding a stout stick in one hand.

"Come on. Let's get out of here," he said.

We ran back to camp.

The two men hadn't seen who cold-cocked them. Sasha was safe. But I knew that men like those two, bad men, count on silence. Shame is their ally. The more silent their victims, the more they can attack other unsuspecting women. Knowing this as I did deep down inside, I stood atop one of the tables near the wood stove and called a meeting, stamping my feet to get attention. Sasha whistled.

As I related what had happened to me, I saw my mother cry and nearly collapse. I saw Donia steady her. I saw the anger in my father and brother rise until it choked them to keep it inside. I could tell that they wanted to hurt those men. They probably wanted to kill them. But doing that would only bring more suffering, more cruelty. Besides, they might get hurt. I assured everyone that I was okay. We agreed that the best thing was that no girl or woman should go the outhouse by herself. Instead, we'd go in groups; the bigger the better. And we'd carry clubs. I saw the pride in Agafon's eyes for the way I was helping the people, protecting them. I saw Peter shake Sasha's hand.

After the meeting, Sasha and I sat on two stumps along an outside wall of the cannery looking at the beautiful red sky. Sasha's club leaned against the wall behind him just in case.

"Red sky at night; sailor's delight," he said.

I nodded and took his hand in mine.

"Thanks for saving me."

"Any time."

Neither of us spoke for a few minutes. We were both thinking about the events of the past hour.

"Your brother thanked me for helping you," said Sasha. "He said I was okay in his book."

"You're okay in my book, too."

"I'm proud of you."

"What for?"

"For being brave. You probably just saved someone."

We were quiet again.

"Some birthday this turned out to be," I grumbled.

Sasha leaned toward me. I pulled back, caught off guard.

He looked into my eyes. I felt safe, like I was home.

Then he kissed me for the first time.

"Happy birthday," he whispered while our lips were still close.

It was the best present I ever got.

CHAPTER 15
Donia

One morning in mid-July I noticed something different about Donia while we were getting dressed in the morning. There was a bump on her usually flat stomach, which certainly couldn't be explained from overeating. There was only one reason I could think of.

My sister was pregnant!

Donia saw me staring at her stomach and placed her finger to her lips and then pointed outside, jabbing her finger excitedly into the air. I could tell by the look in her eyes that she didn't want me to say anything in front of our parents, who were just waking up.

Donia quickly turned and buttoned up her blouse when Mother sat up.

"Good morning, daughters," she said to both of us.

We both said "good morning," and after getting dressed and putting our shoes on, we met outside by the little creek.

"You're pregnant!" I said.

"Not so loud. Someone will hear you," replied Donia looking around to see if anyone overheard.

"I saw your belly. You're going to have a baby."

"Please don't tell Mom and Dad," Donia pleaded.

"You can't hide something like that," I said, pointing to her stomach. "It's just going to get bigger and bigger until it'll be impossible to hide it from anyone."

"I know . . . I just need a little more time to think."

"Think about what?"

"About *how* to tell them . . . *what* to tell them."

"Who's the father?" I asked, even though I feared I already knew her answer.

"It's . . . it's one of the white men."

"A Keeper? The father is one of the Keepers?" I said as if I was surprised. I was sure Donia didn't know I had seen her going into the shed with the white man.

"His name is Patrick. He's very nice to me. He says he loves me . . ."

I couldn't imagine the words *love* and *keeper* in the same sentence. What's more, I had seen how the men paid the women who went into the shed with them. I had never been in love, but I knew that one doesn't pay for love.

"He says he wants me to go with him when the war is over, says he wants to get married."

"Are you going to go with him?" I asked.

"I don't know yet. I need more time to think about it."

"You'll have to tell Mom and Dad soon. You can't keep it a secret much longer."

"I know," said Donia. "Are you going to tell them?"

"No. That's something you have to do," I replied. "But promise me: no more drinking whiskey."

Donia hugged me for a long time. She was crying. I could feel her trembling.

Even though I was concerned for my sister, I understood how she must have felt, what she must be thinking. She had lost so much in the past year, first her husband and then her baby. So much love lost . . . so much sadness. I really couldn't blame her for trying to fill the hole in her heart . . .

Even if it was with a Keeper.

• • • •

With midsummer came the schools of salmon, innumerable as the stars. When the tide came in, salmon raced up the shallow stream pouring into the little cove where I hid my kayak. But I had a hard time trying to catch them. Agafon was no longer strong enough to walk with me, so I described the situation to him while we were sitting outside.

"Make a fish weir," he suggested.

"A what?"

"Pile rocks across creek at two places—one upstream, one downstream—about twenty or thirty feet apart. Leave opening on down-creek side so fish swim in. When tide go out, block opening so fish trapped. Then they easy to catch."

To help me understand better, Agafon drew a picture in the dirt with a stick. It looked like two dams.

"See? Fish swim in here at high tide but can't get out at low tide."

It took me a long time to pile all the rocks across the stream for the two dams, but the labor was well worth it. The really hard part was quickly closing the opening in the lower dam with rocks when the tide was going out. But every time the tide came in and went out, I caught more salmon than I could carry.

• • • •

With so many of the men gone, Sasha returned to speculating on who was catching the salmon. He was obsessed with finding out who it was, and he was still certain that it must be a man. For whatever reason, he narrowed it down to a man named Isodor Philemenoff, whom he followed like an unwanted second shadow for days, certain that Philemenoff was the one secretly catching the fish. It was so funny to watch. I don't even know why Sasha decided that Isodor was the one. He had a bad leg and was blind in one eye. He used a stout stick as a cane to help him walk. Nevertheless, Sasha followed the poor man everywhere, even when he went outside to pee in the woods at night. I have no idea what Isodor must have thought, but I remember the day it stopped. I saw the whole thing.

Sasha was following the man around the camp, trying to be inconspicuous, like a secret agent or something. He trailed him all the way to the outhouse at the end of the dock and back, concealing himself in the forest along the trail so as not to be seen. But I could tell that Isodor knew he was being tailed. Anyone who might have taken any notice could see from Isodor's face that he was annoyed. Sasha was making himself a real nuisance.

From where I was sitting outside the cannery on a stump, I watched as Isodor limped to the tool shed and walked behind it, looking over his shoulder to see if his shadow was following. Predictably, Sasha slunk along a minute later. I saw Isodor work his way around the shed, until he had come back to the front. He pressed himself against the wall and waited. When Sasha came around the corner, thinking he had lost the man, Isodor grabbed him by his red suspenders and pulled him close. I saw them speaking, then Isodor released Sasha and shambled off. When Sasha came over to where I was standing I asked him what the man had said.

"He asked me why I was following him."

"What did you say?" I asked.

"I told him I thought he was the person catching all the salmon."

"Was he?"

"No," replied Sasha, looking embarrassed. "He asked me if I really thought a one-legged man with one eye could sneak past the Keepers and catch fish in the sea?"

"Sounds reasonable to me," I chuckled.

I don't think Sasha saw the humor.

CHAPTER 16
Kiska, Seal Hunter

The next day was perfect weather for seal hunting. I left early in the morning. I was out in my kayak well before most at the cannery were wide awake. Father and Uncle were always saying how seals and sea otters don't give themselves to the lazy hunter who sleeps in late or who complains about the cold.

Rounding a point, I saw five seals sunning on a rookery. I planned my approach, coming up from behind the rocks, so they wouldn't see me until it was too late. I paddled quietly, with long, slow strokes that went deep. As the kayak glided silently closer, I heard the seals barking on the other side of the rocks. I waited for the wind to be in my favor, and then I edged around the rocks, careful not to let the paddle scrape the side of the kayak for fear of making noise. When I was close, I set down the paddle and picked up my spear. As I drifted toward them, the seals burst into commotion, frantically trying to heave their bodies across the uneven rock and into the water.

This time I waited to throw my spear. I was learning one of the most important lessons of hunting: patience.

One by one they plunged into the sea. Four of the seals surfaced far away, but one—the one who gave himself to me—surfaced just in front of the nose of my kayak. Without hesitation I cocked my arm back and aimed. I had heard Father and Uncle and the other men back home say never to spear a seal or sea otter near the tail. They said a seal hit that way will not die and will fight vigorously. I aimed for just below the neck and hurled the spear.

The shaft flew straight and true.

I had killed my first seal. I was out on the sea in a kayak that I had made myself, and I had successfully stalked and killed my first seal. I knew that Agafon would be proud. I wished I could have told my father.

I tied the sleek, dead animal to my kayak and paddled back to the little cove, where I cut up the meat, filling two old gray pails I had stored beneath a pile of driftwood. I pulled my kayak up into the forest and turned it upside down, as I always did and covered it with spruce boughs and brush. I lugged the heavy pails of meat back to camp, stopping often to relieve the ache in my arms and back.

When I arrived, I crept up to one of the open windows in the kitchen area where I knew there was a counter just inside the window. I looked around, making sure no one saw me. No one was nearby, though I could see a lot of people standing at the far end of the cannery with their backs to me. I hoisted the pails one at a time and pushed them onto the table where they would be found. Then I walked around to the front of the building, whistling happily.

Sasha ran up to me. I could tell he was excited.

"Where have you been?"

"Oh, around," I lied. "Why? What's going on?"

"Agafon had a heart attack! He's been asking for you," Sasha said as he took me by the arm and led me into the cannery to where Agafon lay on the plank floor covered with a green blanket, his head resting on a wadded up jacket. His eyes were closed and he looked pale. I thought he was dead. I knelt beside him and took his hand.

"I'm here," I said.

Agafon's eye's fluttered open.

"I glad you here," he said weakly.

I wanted to tell him about the seal, but there were people standing around, including Mother and Father. I leaned close and whispered in his ear.

"I got a seal. The magic amulet worked."

Despite his condition, Agafon smiled and patted my hand.

"I proud of you. If I had granddaughter, she be just like you."

Even now, I remember how much his words meant to me. They still do, even after all these years.

"You're not alone anymore. I'm your family," I said and then kissed his forehead.

"I need tell you something," he said slowly between long breaths. Then he closed his eyes.

I could tell that Agafon's life was slipping away.

"Stay with me," I said.

Agafon opened his eyes again and tenderly squeezed my hand. There was so little strength left in him.

"No magic," he said. "It always been you."

"But you said the amulet had magic."

"I say that for you own good."

I laughed and wiped tears from my cheeks. For a few minutes Agafon struggled to breathe.

"Closer," he was finally able to whisper.

I placed my ear to his lips.

"Thank . . . you . . ." he murmured. After a brief pause his body stiffened and his face grimaced as if he were in pain. I held his hand tighter. But then his tortured body relaxed, and I heard the air in his lungs go out for the last time. I lay my head on his still chest and wept.

"Please don't go," I pleaded, still holding his hand.

But it was too late.

• • • •

We buried Agafon in the crowded little cemetery. Father, Uncle, Peter, and Sasha helped me dig his grave. Mother and Donia sang a hymn and helped me pick a bouquet of wild flowers. When we were done, I asked to be left alone. After the others had left, Father stopped and hugged me.

"He was your friend."

"Yes," I replied meekly, remembering my father's stern warning to stay away from Agafon.

My father hugged me again as I sobbed against his chest.

I sat by Agafon's grave for a long time until it was late, my arms around my knees, my head resting on my arms. I must have dozed off a couple of times. When I was ready to leave it was so late that nearly everyone back in the cannery must have been asleep.

"Goodbye," I said when I got up to leave, wiping my cheeks.

An owl hooted in the distance.

When I walked into camp, Sasha was waiting for me.

"For you," he said, holding out something wrapped in a red-and-white-checkered cloth.

"What is it?"

"It's a chunk of seal meat," replied Sasha. "While we were digging the grave, someone discovered two buckets full of seal meat, enough for everyone. Our mystery hunter has been busy again. We had a feast, roasting the meat on sticks over a campfire. I saved you a piece."

I think the circumstances prevented Sasha, once again, from connecting me in any way with the secret provider. As far as he knew, I was with him digging Agafon's grave when the buckets were discovered.

Sasha led me by the hand to the fire pit ringed by tree stumps. The embers were still glowing. He added a few pieces of wood and blew at the base until the flames jumped up. Then he handed me a roasting stick, and we stared at the mesmerizing flames licking the dark meat, both of us thinking.

"I'm sorry about your friend," Sasha said. "I'm glad I got a chance to know him a little."

"Thanks."

Then we were quiet again.

When I thought the seal was cooked enough I took a bite.

"It's delicious," I said. "It tastes like home."

• • • •

Everyone was happy when the men returned from the Pribilofs a few days later. We had been so vulnerable in their absence. They say there's strength and safety in numbers. I can tell you it's true. There was a good deal of talk about what had happened to me. There was a lot of tension between our men and the Keepers for a couple days until the two men who had tried to rape me were quietly reassigned to another camp, shipped out in the dead of night. After that things returned to normal.

But not everything returned to normal.

After the terrifying incident in the kayak and the loss of Agafon, I began to have terrible nightmares. I dreamed that the giant, unseen fish pulled me far out to sea, away from everything I had ever known, and the further it took me, the more the world turned black and empty—a great nothingness. No more island, no more village, no more cannery, no more family. Nothing. Ghosts of the dead haunted me in the blackness— Umma, Agafon, even Mary. There were so many of them, circling me, shrieking silently at me, their contorting mouths like toothless black holes.

I awoke night after night drenched in sweat, my heart pounding so hard I could feel it against the plank floor.

CHAPTER 17
Home

The rest of summer and fall passed much as they did the first year, with all of us trying to get by as best we could. I continued to supplement our diet, as best I could, with food from the sea, secretly. I had learned how to do that. I had learned how to help others, as Agafon had taught me. I never did get another seal, though I came close a couple times.

I remember that a dead beluga whale had washed up on the beach in the little cove where I kept my kayak. For almost a week, bears came to feed on it. I avoided them for the most part. But one day I must have surprised a bear sleeping in dense brush. I was dragging my kayak from its hiding place down to the pebbly beach through dense brush when the bear stood up on its hind legs. It must have been eight or nine feet tall, maybe more. It dropped to all fours and starting shaking its shaggy head, snarling, and baring its yellow teeth.

I was terrified.

I pulled out my little pocketknife and clutched it tightly in my right hand as the bear took a menacing lunge at me. I backed up, tripping over my kayak. The bear was just about to charge me when Peter burst out from the bushes with a stout club in his hand, more log than stick. He stood in front of me, shouting madly and waving his arms.

I think Peter surprised the bear. It stopped in its tracks.

"Get up and yell!" Peter turned and shouted to me. "Whatever you do, don't run."

I got up on my feet and started yelling too.

"Go away! Get out of here!"

I don't remember what I said; I just know that I screamed it at the top of my lungs. I was so scared. At one point, I picked up a rock and threw it at the bear, hitting it on the shoulder. I don't think he even noticed.

At first the bear snapped at Peter, but eventually it turned and ambled off toward the decaying whale down the beach.

It took a few minutes for our nerves to calm and to stop trembling.

"What are you doing here?" I asked.

"I followed you. I saw you sneak out of camp, and I wondered where you were going. What are you doing here?" asked Peter, looking at the kayak behind me.

I didn't have to say a word.

"Holy cow! *You're* the one catching all the food."

"Please don't tell anyone."

"My little sister, the rebel."

"Please," I repeated. "You can't say anything to anyone."

"Why not?"

I told my brother what Agafon had told me about keeping my activities secret, about how Mr. Anderson and the others would stop me if they found out, how our people would suffer without the extra food to stay strong.

"You've been doing this for over a year?" he asked.

I nodded, smiling.

I told Peter about everything I had done, even about the giant fish that had pulled me out to sea.

A serious look fell across Peter's smiling face.

"You could have got hurt. That bear could have killed you if I hadn't come along," he said.

"I know. Thanks."

But then the smile returned to his face.

"You got a seal all by yourself," Peter marveled, shaking his head as if he couldn't believe it.

But deep down inside he knew it was true.

"Does Sasha know?" he asked.

"Nope," I said. "He thinks it's you."

Peter chuckled.

"I still can't believe it's you. I'm proud of you, Little Sister."

I could tell my brother was sincerely proud of me and what he perceived as my little act of resistance. But to me, what I had been doing wasn't about resisting or rebellion—it was about *helping*, the way Agafon and Father had taught me.

I asked Peter to promise that he wouldn't tell anyone. He agreed to keep my secret. We decided it was too dangerous for me to go out in my kayak while the bears were around. Instead, I beachcombed elsewhere at low tide for mussels and clams and gumboots—a kind of edible snail, delicious once you get a taste for them. There's a saying in our culture: "The table is set when the tide goes out."

True to his word, Peter never told a living soul about finding out it was me.

· · · ·

One day Mr. Anderson told us that we were going home.

He said a ship would arrive within a few days to take us back to our villages. I wonder if you can imagine how happy we were. After our long imprisonment . . . I mean *internment* . . . we were finally going home. We had little to do to prepare for our departure—nothing to pack, no possessions to speak of, and no need to clean the place. It was already in better condition than when we arrived, thanks to our hard work. Our best memory of the cannery would be watching it vanish into the distance as the ship steamed away.

The last thing I did before we left was to say goodbye to Agafon and my Umma.

"I won't forget my promise," I said to my grandmother as I stood between their graves.

"Thank you for helping me, for helping everyone," I said to Agafon. "I won't forget what you taught me. You may have been alone all your life, but I'll never forget you. You're part of my family now."

• • • •

Donia didn't board the ship with us. She went with her soldier on a different ship. We got a postcard from San Francisco about a year later. It had a picture of the Golden Gate Bridge. Donia's brief scribbled message didn't even mention a baby or a wedding. We never heard from her again. I don't know where she is or if she's even alive.

The trip home aboard the ship took as long as it did when it brought us to internment. From the ship deck we could see airfields and docks and hillside bunkers that hadn't existed before, the visible evidence of war. But unlike our uncertain voyage to Funter Bay, our return trip was filled with the happiness of anticipation of going home. But our happiness was short-lived. Half the villages had been burned to the ground. For the people of those villages, there was nothing to go home to. The ship stopped at each of the villages on the way, letting off the people who lived there. Most of the villages had lost ten to fifteen percent of their population; some lost more than a quarter.

When we arrived at Sasha's village, we could see stacks of building supplies at the end of the dock: lumber and doors and windows, sinks and stoves and roofing metal—everything needed to rebuild their burned down homes. Sasha lingered until everyone else had disembarked down the long metal gangway. We hugged for a long time at the bottom, uncertain if we'd ever meet again.

"We'll see each other again," said Sasha.

"Yes. We'll find a way."

"We can write letters."

"Yes . . . letters," I nodded sadly, knowing it would never be the same.

Eventually, a sailor told us that the ship would weigh anchor in a few minutes and I that had better get back aboard if I wanted to go home.

"I'm glad you were there," I said to Sasha. "You made it bearable."

"*I'm* glad *you* were there," replied Sasha, his eyes beginning to tear. It was the first time I ever saw him cry.

We kissed goodbye.

Only the sailor standing at the top of the gangway saw us.

I was just about to tell Sasha that I loved him when another sailor shouted down to me to get aboard.

From the back of the ship—the long white wake connecting our breaking hearts—I watched Sasha standing on the dock until he became as small and as distant as a fading memory. Then I saw him turn and walk away.

I never felt so alone.

I cried all the way home.

There were few of us left aboard by the time the ship arrived at our island. From a couple miles out we could see our houses and our beautiful church with its blue steeple. For my family, we at least had the joy of knowing that our village had not been destroyed. Our home was waiting for us exactly the way we had left it. We would pick up our lives as if the past months were but a bad dream. We grew so excited. But when we landed all of our excitement turned to despair. The view from a distance had been deceiving. In reality, our village was in shambles. All of our homes had been ransacked and vandalized. The doors and windows were broken. Left open to the weather, the walls were green with mold; wallpaper hung off the walls like tongues. Plates and glass and family pictures were shattered on the floor. Jewelry, cash, and hunting rifles had all been stolen. In an act of senseless vandalism, the fragile outer skins on all of the baidarkas had been slashed to pieces. Flaps of skin waved in the wind like tattered ghosts.

We didn't have much to begin with.

Now we had nothing.

Worst of all, our beloved church had been looted. All of the beautiful things had been stolen, all of candlesticks and censors and gold-framed icons. The pews had been torn out and burned in a bonfire outside. Bibles and hymnals lay in the ashes. The windows were shattered, the walls were riddled with bullet holes, and the steeple had been shot up, apparently for target practice. The golden cross had been cut in half by machine gun fire. The top portion lay broken on the ground.

But it wasn't the Japanese who had destroyed our village.

We were later told that American soldiers had been billeted in our homes during the war. They had shot up our village from boredom. They burned the pews for entertainment. And when they were ordered to leave the islands after the Japanese had been defeated, they stole anything of value or as a souvenir.

Years later, we learned that the government had even lied to us about the seal harvest in the Pribilofs that summer. Not one fur was used to keep pilots and airmen warm as they fought the good fight. Instead, we learned that the furs had been sold for cash, $1,500,000 in fact. Our men had been forced to labor for someone else's profit like slaves . . . No, as slaves. They say the war was fought to protect freedom, but *our* freedom was taken from us. Even after all these years, it's hard for me to comprehend the war and what happened to us.

I remember how we all somehow ended up in the empty church that evening. We wept when my father carried in the heavy broken cross on his shoulder and leaned it against the altar. Even Peter, for all his toughness, had to wipe his face. We held hands and sang hymns, the rising wind singing through the broken windows.

· · · ·

"Well, there you have it. That's the story I wanted to tell you, Granddaughter. Telling it has made me tired. It comes with getting old."

"Did you ever go back to the cannery, Grandmother?"

"I did. When your mother was about your age, I went back and brought my Umma home. True to my promise, I buried her beside my Uppa in the cemetery behind our church. I also brought Agafon here. He's buried beside my grandparents."

"I always wondered who that was."

"Now you know. He's part of our family. Remember him and what he did for us. Will you help me clean the table? Put the tea cups and plates in the sink. The sugar bowl goes in the cupboard to the right of the stove."

"Is this good, Grandmother?"

"Very good. You're so helpful. I'm glad you came to visit me and to hear my story. Now you know that I once had a sister and that you are named after her. I told you this story because it's part of who we are, who *you* are. We carry the past with us, the good and the bad. It makes us into who we are. Your great uncle Peter learned that. He turned his anger and outrage about what happened to us into something positive. He went to college and became a lawyer. He tirelessly fought injustice, and he never stopped fighting to protect our lands and our rights, right up to the very end."

"I miss Uncle Peter."

"I miss him, too. But everyone's time comes. Peter was almost eighty when his time came. Mine is not far off."

"You're not old, Umma."

"How sweet of you to say that. You have a big heart. I don't know if you're old enough to understand all of the things I've shared with you, but maybe one day you will see it clearly. What you do with the story now is up to you. See that little wooden box on the shelf? Yes, that one. Bring it to me, please. I've waited a long time to give you this. I think you are now old enough."

"What is it?"

"Open it and you'll see."

"A pocketknife!"

"It's the one Agafon gave me. I'm giving it to you."

"It's beautiful."

"Please be careful with it. It's still very sharp. Take out the piece of cloth. There's something inside I want to give you."

"It's a sea lion! Is it the necklace Agafon made for you?"

"Yes, Little One. It's yours now. I don't know if it has magic or not, but it helped me to find courage. Now it will help you, too."

"Thank you, Grandmother!"

"What a nice hug. I love your hugs. I warned you that this was a heartbreaking story and that it would be hard to bear. I can't forget all the people we lost, all the cruelty and needless suffering. Some pains time cannot erase. But if I have learned anything over the years, it's that life is for the living. Yesterday is only a shadow. The sun only shines on today. Live fully in every moment, Granddaughter. Live without fear. That is the purpose of the story in your life. Never give up, no matter how hard life becomes. And remember to help others on their journey. Find the way that only *you* can help others. Find who you are. That's important. Promise me you'll do these things."

"I promise."

"Such a sweet, smart girl. Listen! I hear your Uppa is up from his nap. He never did find out that I was the one who caught all the food. Please don't say anything to him. Here he comes now."

"Grandpa Sasha!"

EPILOGUE

The Japanese invasion of Alaska never made it very far beyond the westernmost Aleutian Islands of Kiska and Attu. Over a period of fifteen months, American soldiers eventually recaptured the mountainous islands in a series of battles which came to be known as "The Forgotten War". In all, half a million soldiers—American, Canadian, Russian, and Japanese—were involved in the conflict, one of the least known yet toughest-fought battles in WWII. In proportion to the number of troops involved, the battle to recapture the tiny weather-beaten island of Attu ranks as the second most costly American battle in the Pacific Theater, second only to Iwo Jima. Some of the most horrific accounts of hand-to-hand combat in World War II happened at the end when over five hundred Japanese soldiers, refusing to surrender or to be taken alive after a desperate Banzai attack, blew themselves up en masse with hand grenades at the foot of Engineer Hill (read Russell Annabel's remarkable story in his book, *Alaskan Adventures*).

The war in the Aleutians gave America her first theater-wide victory over Japan and the first experience at amphibious assaults in the war, which prepared America for future island invasions in the Pacific as well as for D-Day. The seven hundred German prisoners—sworn enemies of America—all returned home after the war. Not one of them died during their imprisonment, while over one hundred Aleuts perished from lack of warmth, food, and medical care. Some of the smaller villages lost as much as a quarter of their pre-internment population. The deaths were avoidable. Medical supplies that had been allocated for the internment camps were instead taken by the military. For decades, the little cemetery in the ravine behind the cannery was in disrepair, overgrown and mostly forgotten, but it was recently improved with new markers and new crosses (see photograph at end of this section).

Although the Japanese invasion was defeated by the fall of 1943, the Aleuts remained interned until the end of the war in 1945. In 1980, President Reagan signed the Commission on Wartime Relocation and Internment of Civilians Act, which authorized the establishment of a commission to review the facts and circumstances surrounding the relocation and internment of tens of thousands of American civilians—mostly Japanese-Americans and Aleutian Islanders—during World War II under Executive Order 9066, as well as to review directives of United States military forces requiring the relocation and internment of American civilians.

Forty-two years after the Aleuts returned to their

burned and ransacked villages, the United States government finally recognized that their constitutional rights had been violated. In 1988, Congress passed the Aleut Restitution Act (P.L. 100-383), which paid a mere $12,000 to surviving victims of the internment camps. By then, unfortunately, about half of the survivors had long since passed away. United States Senator Ted Stevens (R, Alaska)—the longest-serving republican senator in American history and President pro tempore of the senate (Third in Line for Presidential succession)—co-sponsored the landmark bill.

In 1986, Sen. Stevens asked John Smelcer, a cultural anthropologist and oral historian, to interview surviving Aleut elders so that their heartrending stories could be included in the legislation. (Photo of John Smelcer and Sen. Ted Stevens in Copper Center, Alaska, 1996, courtesy Zara Smelcer)

The story and character of Kiska is based on a real person who died many years ago. She was older than Kiska is in the story. She said that no one ever discovered that it was she who had helped her people during the internment at Funter Bay, and she asked that it remain that way. She never considered herself a hero. As far as she was concerned, she did what she had to do given the circumstance. "People were hungry," she used to say to me. "So I helped." This story is intended to represent the Aleut internment experience—not that of a single person, group, or place.

Photographs

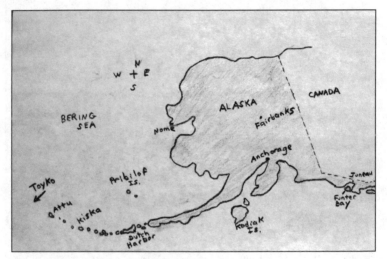

Drawing by John Smelcer

Aleutian villagers being transported to the
USS Delarof on small boats.
Alaska State Library, Butler/Dale Photo Collection, P306-1091

Aleut woman washing dishes at Internment camp.
Alaska State Library, Butler/Dale Photo Collection, P306-1094

Aleut children in front of Ward lake sign.
Alaska State Library, Butler/Dale Photo Collection, P306-1044

German POW camp Kantine.
Alaska State Library, U.S. Army Signal Corps Photo Collection,
P175-115

German POW camp living quarters.
Alaska State Library, U.S. Army Signal Corps Photo Collection,
P175-114

German POW camp mess hall.
Alaska State Library, U.S. Army Signal Corps Photo Collection,
P175-119

Questions for Discussion

Chapter 1

1. Look at the map of the Aleutian Chain in the Photographs section. Note how long it is, how remote, and how far it stretches across the Pacific Ocean toward Japan. The farthest island, Attu, is five time zones away from the state capitol in Juneau.
2. Describe Kiska's island and her village.
3. Although Kiska's father says girls aren't allowed to hunt, Kiska wants to be a hunter like her father someday so that she too can provide for her family and community. What do you think about her aspiration?
4. What did Kiska say to her older sister, Donia, to help her through her grief?
5. After listening to her uncle retell the myth about the first seals, Kiska wonders about its meaning. What do you think about the story?
6. In what way is Kiska's father's comment "a storm's coming" foreshadowing?
7. How significant is the Russian Orthodox Church in the community?
8. What is the legacy of the Russian-American period in Alaska?

Chapter 2

1. In 1942, Alaska Natives were American citizens, even though Alaska was not yet a state. What do you think of the way they were treated? Did the

soldiers have to burn the villages and kill all the cats and dogs? Couldn't they have at least waited until the villagers couldn't see it? The colonel told them this was "for their own good." What do you think about that?

2. How is the plight of the Aleuts in the hold similar to that of Africans during their trans-Atlantic journey to become slaves in the Americas?

3. Knowing that this story is based on true historical events, what do you think of the ship doctor who wouldn't help the sick Aleuts in the ship's hold? Although the government stated that they were acting in the Aleut's best interest, what do you think of the policy and the way it was executed?

Chapter 3

1. Describe how alien and inhospitable the Southeast Alaska rainforest must have seemed to the Aleuts. How would you feel if you were suddenly dropped off in someplace foreign?

2. Describe the appalling condition of the abandoned cannery at Funter Bay. In selecting the site as an internment camp, do you think the government gave much consideration to the comfort and basic needs of the Aleut?

3. Although the Aleuts were told they were not prisoners, Kiska said that she felt as if she were. What do you think?

4. Some readers may think Kiska to be passive. Giv-

en all that happened to her, and the suddenness of it all at gunpoint, what do you think? How would you have reacted?

Chapter 4
1. Discuss the disparity between the decrepit living conditions of the Aleuts and that of the camp superintendent and his staff.

Chapter 5
1. What do you think about Peter's assertion that the Aleuts are prisoners who should resist their imprisonment? Do you think the Aleuts had become too accepting of their internment?

Chapter 6
1. Agafon's backstory is incredible, yet it's historically true that contact with Russians brought disease and plagues to the Aleuts (indeed to many Alaska Natives), decimating their population throughout the island chain (and elsewhere across Alaska). What is it that Agafon sees in Kiska, and what do you think he is asking her to do?

Chapter 7
1. Although Germany was the sworn enemy of the United States, having turned Europe and Russia into a wasteland of destruction and ruin, killing American soldiers and merchant sailors, and millions of civilians, and enslaving and slaughtering

millions of Jews and raping millions of Russian women, the German prisoner-of-war camp at Excursion Bay was far more comfortable than the Aleut internment camp, even though the Aleuts were American citizens who had done nothing to deserve their imprisonment. Indeed, one historian wrote, "all in all, the German imprisonment in Alaska was quite pleasant." How do you account for that?

2. Kiska seems to have made up her mind to do something to help her people. What do you think she's going to do?

Chapter 8
1. Do you think a good diet is important for health and well-being?
2. Why do you think Agafon teaches Kiska how to fish instead of doing it himself?
3. How is Kiska breaking with tradition to help her people?

Chapter 9
1. Discuss the *irony* that although Agafon is the most ostracized member of the community— shunned as an outcast throughout his life—it is he who helps save the People by mentoring Kiska.
2. What does Kiska's grandmother ask her to do after she dies?
3. How is Kiska's comment about the cemetery foreshadowing?

Chapter 10

1. Discuss the irony of Kiska helping Sasha to discover whoever it is catching food for the community.
2. Kiska and Sasha have a lively debate about gender roles. To what degree does gender still define or limit roles in society? How does your gender define you?
3. To learn more about the amazing story of Millie and Maura, read John Smelcer's award-winning novel *The Great Death*.
4. It is absolutely true that white men plied the young, naïve Aleut women with alcohol for sexual favors. There are photographs of camp staff receiving cases of chocolate bars.

Chapter 11
1. What would you do if a giant fish was pulling you far out to sea in a tiny boat?
2. Although Kiska had been providing fish for her people, why does the notion of seal meat excite Agafon? Do you think it will be easy for Kiska to hunt seals?

Chapter 12
1. Kiska tells us that the soldiers often called the Aleuts animals, saying that they weren't really human beings. She also points out that the young white soldiers didn't seem to think that when they met secretly met with Aleut women in the tool shed. How do you explain this dichotomy?

Can you compare this attitude to other periods in history?

Chapter 13

1. It is a historical fact that diseases carried by white people have devastated indigenous populations worldwide, especially during the colonization of the Americas, Africa, and Australia and New Zealand. 118 Aleuts at Funter Bay contracted measles. Many died from it, mostly the very young and the very old. The cemetery is still there. Why do you think the Aleuts were so susceptible to measles? Why do you think Agafon didn't contract measles? Why didn't a single Keeper get sick? Have you been inoculated against this once common disease?

2. How do you feel about the soldier's assertion that God was punishing the Aleuts?

Chapter 14

1. It is a fact that the government threatened that none of the Aleuts would ever be allowed to go home if the men didn't "volunteer" to harvest fur seals for the war effort. What is equally true is that the government lied. The skins were not used as liners for aviation jackets or helmets for our pilots, which might have made the Pribilovian men proud for their little contribution to winning the war. Instead, the profits from the seal harvest, $1,500,000 went straight into the government's

coffers. How do you feel about the deception?

2. Discuss the irony of how Mr. Anderson uses phrases like "your government," "Uncle Sam," and "volunteer like good Americans" when announcing the government's ultimatum.

3. In interviews, many Aleut women related how white men at the camps plied them with liquor for sex. Alcoholism became a severe problem for many Aleuts even after their internment. After reading this chapter, do you think the Aleuts needed protection from their protectors?

4. Do you think Kiska did the right thing by telling everyone what had happened to her? Why do you think many young women would never do what she did?

Chapter 15

1. Many women got pregnant by soldiers during WWII, often with the phony promise of love and marriage. How do you think the future bodes for Donia and her baby?

Chapter 16

1. With his dying breath, Agafon thanks Kiska. Why is he thanking her?

Chapter 17

1. Why do you think Kiska tells her granddaughter the story of what happened during World War II and gives her the sea lion necklace even though

she knows it has no magic?

2. Sasha never did discover that Kiska was the one who had provided the food at Funter Bay. Do you think he should be told?

3. Ostensibly, the United States government wanted to protect the Aleuts from the possibility that Japanese forces might have continued their invasion of the Aleutian Islands. Those captured would likely have been killed or transported to Japan as prisoners of war. In the end, after all their suffering, and nearly a hundred deaths by a disease contracted from their jailors, and after the senseless destruction of their villages and churches by American soldiers, not by the enemy, did the United States protect the Aleuts?

4. Peter is impulsive while Kiska is more deliberate. Yet, in their own way, both Kiska and Peter confound the Keepers with small acts of rebellion and resistance. How are their actions similar? How are they different?

5. In the years after internment, how did Peter use his rebellious nature to fight injustice? Do you think his experience at Funter Bay played a role in his future career path?

6. Does learning that Kiska is based on a real person affect how you feel about the story?

Resources for Further Studies

www.wikipedia.org/wiki/Aleutian-Islands-Campaign

www.wikipedia.org/wiki/Aleut_people

www.apiai.org/culture-history/history/

[the website of the Aleutian Pribilof Islands Association, Inc.]

http://akhistorycourse.org/articles/article.php?artID=215

[Alaska History and Cultural Studies: The Aleut Evacuation]

"The Other WWII American-Internment Atrocity," by John Smelcer. Published on NPR:

http://www.npr.org/sections/codeswitch/2017/02/21/516277507/the-other-wwii-american-internment-atrocity

Aleut Evacuation [video] 1992. (60 minutes, color)

Aleut Story [video] 2005. (90 minutes, color) www.aleutstory.tv

Learn more about the documentary at http://usatoday30.usatoday.com/news/nation/2005-12-04-aleut_x.htm?csp=34

Unangam Ungiikangin Kayux Tunusangin: Aleut Tales and Narratives [book] edited by

Knut Bergsland and Moses Dirks. Fairbanks: ANLC/UAF, 1990.

The Raven and the Totem: Alaska Native Myths and Legends [book] edited by John Smelcer.

Various publishers: 1991, 2015 (2nd edition).

When the Wind Was a River [book] by Dean Kohlhoff. Seattle: University of Washington, 1995.

Ghosts in the Fog [book] by Samantha Seiple. New York: Scholastic, 2011.

Alaskan Adventures: Early Years [book] by Russell Annabel (read the chapter "Sportsmen

with Silver Wings"). Long Beach: Safari Press, 1997.

The Forgotten War: A Pictorial History of World War II in Alaska [book] by Stan Cohen.

Missoula: Pictorial Histories Publishing, 1988.

The Thousand-Mile War: World War II in Alaska and the Aleutians [book] by Brian Garfield.

New York: Ballantine, 1969; reprinted by the University of Alaska Press, 1995.

To learn more about the devastating effects of epidemics on Alaska Natives, read John Smelcer's acclaimed novel *The Great Death* (2006) and Harold Napoleon's *Yuuyaraq: The Way of the Human Being* (1996). To learn more about the amazing true story of Ada Blackjack, read Jennifer Niven's *Ada Blackjack: A True Story of Survival in the Arctic* (2003).

About the Author

A member of the Ahtna tribe of Alaska, John Smelcer served as executive director of the Ahtna Heritage Foundation, compiling and editing *The Ahtna Noun Dictionary and Pronunciation Guide*. He has done archaeological surveys throughout Ahtna's tribal lands. He later served as the director of Chenega Native Corporation's Language and Cultural Preservation Project, working with elders to compile *The Alutiiq Noun Dictionary and Pronunciation Guide* and editing *The Day That Cries Forever* and *We are the Land, We are the Sea*.

Also from Leapfrog Press

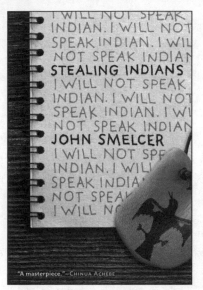

"A masterpiece." —Chinua Achebe

Stealing Indians

John Smelcer

1950: Four Indian teens from different regions of America are forcibly taken from their families and shipped to a faraway boarding school where their lives will be immutably changed by an institution designed to eradicate their identity. And no matter what their home, their stories are representative of every story, every stolen life. So far from home, without family to protect them, only their friendship helps them endure. This is a work of fiction. Every word is true.

"Smelcer's anger about these stolen children is apparent but controlled . . . a well-judged balance of horror and hope, with the friendship among his protagonists giving the book heart."
—*Horn Book*

Savage Mountain

John Smelcer

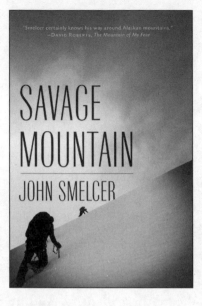

In the summer of 1980, brothers Sebastian and James Savage decide to climb one of the highest mountains in Alaska to prove themselves to their father, a tough and un-loving man who has always belittled them. The brothers, always at odds, develop different ways of coping with this rejection, but each yearns to finally have his respect. Inspired by true events, this story is not about father-son reconciliation. Some relationships can never be mended. Instead, it's a touching story of two brothers who test their limits and realize, finally, that their worth is not dictated by their father, and that no matter how different they might be, the strongest bond of all is brotherhood.

"Set in the interior of Alaska, this novel balances family dynamics, brother-bonding, and high-stakes adventure. . . . The mountaineering and Alaskan drama is both realistic and exotic, suspenseful, and exciting. . . . Extreme adventure sequences and the strong brotherly relationship make this a solid general purchase."
—*School Library Journal*

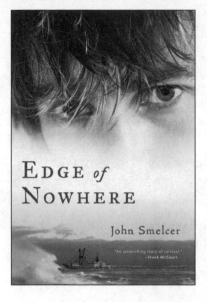

Edge of Nowhere

John Smelcer

Sixteen-year-old Seth and his dog fall off his father's commercial fishing boat in Prince William Sound. They struggle to survive off land and sea as they work their way home from island to island in a three-month journey. The isolation allows Seth to understand his father's love, accept his Native Alaskan heritage, and accept his grief over his mother's death.

"Smelcer's prose is lyrical, straightforward, and brilliant . . . authentic Native Alaskan storytelling at its best."
—*School Library Journal*, starred review

"A spare tale of courage, love and terrible obstacles . . . may have special appeal to teens who like to wonder how they would do if they had to survive in the wild."
—*Wall Street Journal*

"Brief, thoughtful, and often lyrical, this is a quick pick

for young teens who have the good sense not to confuse a short book with a shallow book."
—*Bulletin of the Center for Children's Books*

"More psychological depth than Robinson Crusoe."
—Frank McCourt

Chosen for the 2014 Battle of the Books by the Alaska Association of School Libraries

An American Booksellers Association ABC Best Books for Children title

Lone Wolves
John Smelcer

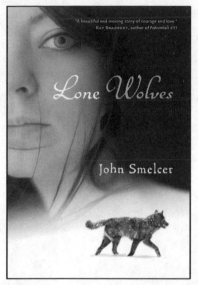

Deneena Yazzie isn't like other 16-year-old girls in her village. Her love of the woods and trail come from her grandfather, who teaches her the all-but-vanished Native Alaskan language and customs. While her peers lose hope, trapped between the old and the modern cultures, Denny and her mysterious lead dog, a blue-eyed wolf, train for the Great Race—a thousand-mile test of courage and endurance through the vast Alaskan wilderness. Denny learns the value of intergenerational friendships, of maintaining connections to her heritage, and of being true to herself, and in her strength she gives her village a new pride and hope.

"With this inspiring young adult novel, Smelcer promises to further solidify his status as 'Alaska's modern-day Jack London.'"
—*Mushing* magazine, Suzanne Steinert

"Powerful, eloquent, and fascinating, showcasing a vanishing way of life in rich detail."
—*Kirkus*

"An engaging tale of survival, love, and courage."
—*School Library Journal*

Amelia Bloomer List of recommended feminist literature
(American Library Association)

Links

Visit Leapfrog Press on Facebook
Google: Facebook Leapfrog Press
or enter:
https://www.facebook.com/pages/Leap-
frog-Press/222784181103418

Leapfrog Press Website
www.leapfrogpress.com

Author Website
www.johnsmelcer.com